# THE FALL OF BLACKSTONE MANSION

## THE BLACKSTONE TRILOGY BOOK 3
## AUGUSTINE PIERCE

PIERCE PUBLISHING

Get your free book, *Zoe's Haunt*, by joining Augustine Pierce's newsletter. You can unsubscribe at any time.

Copyright © 2023 by Augustine Pierce

All rights reserved.

No portion of this book may be reproduced in any form without written permission from the publisher or author, except as permitted by U.S. copyright law.

## Contents

| | |
|---|---:|
| 1 | 1 |
| 2 | 10 |
| 3 | 20 |
| 4 | 35 |
| 5 | 46 |
| 6 | 56 |
| 7 | 68 |
| 8 | 76 |
| 9 | 86 |
| 10 | 93 |
| 11 | 109 |
| 12 | 121 |
| 13 | 136 |
| 14 | 150 |
| 15 | 157 |
| 16 | 168 |

| | |
|---|---|
| 17 | 176 |
| 18 | 183 |
| 19 | 193 |
| 20 | 207 |
| 21 | 221 |
| 22 | 232 |
| 23 | 249 |
| 24 | 261 |
| Free Book! | 276 |
| Acknowledgements | 277 |
| Dark Realm | 278 |
| Also by Augustine Pierce | 279 |
| About the Author | 280 |

# 1

"Beam me up, baby!" Katherine shouted with her hands cupped around her exuberant smile. She knew using that pun was about as far from hip as she could get, but she didn't care. She was in a silly mood this fine Friday evening, and besides, Kirk, her deliciously cute boyfriend, always introduced himself as "like the captain," so she figured if he was going to do it...

Her dark, wavy hair bounced all over her shoulders as she jumped up and down in front of the stage. Every few seconds, the frantic concert lighting danced across her face, making her sea-blue eyes sparkle.

She was at the shoebox-sized Le Soleil club in the Reed College area of southeast Portland, Oregon. The establishment consisted of the stage, large enough for half a band, and standing room for maybe twenty more people. There was also a combination bar and snack counter, and that was it.

# AUGUSTINE PIERCE

She was there to support Kirk, who was on drums for the funk-blues-rock outfit Rodekill. While she wasn't a giant fan of the name, she had to admit that it was far superior to a previous incarnation, the Dolphins, which Kirk's coworker, Shane, had alerted her to during a job several weeks ago. It was during that job, even before Katherine and Kirk had started dating, that she'd told him she'd love to see him play. While she had been flirting, it was also a sincere request.

The job had been the first step in her assessing, moving, and selling the antiques of Blackstone mansion, a massive, abandoned house hidden away in the foothills, about ten minutes' drive from the town of the same name. She'd talked her way into the position with the estate's owner, Jordan Blackstone, a spoiled rich kid by day and part-time DJ by night.

*Ug, Jordan.* He'd been an enormous pain in her ass since the day she'd first spoken to him, from his capricious whims regarding what to do with the mansion to his tendency to threaten to send his lawyers after her whenever he was in a cranky mood. Which was often.

One whim included an almost completely impromptu Halloween party held at the house, tossed together only the previous week, after which she'd been temporarily hospitalized for three days. Amid

# THE FALL OF BLACKSTONE MANSION

the party's chaos, three Blackstone family spirits, those of Gloria, Vernon, and Reginald, had thrust upon Katherine visions of their last moments in life and, after enduring the nightmarish experiences, she'd woken up in an ambulance, with Kirk at her side.

Jordan, of course, knew nothing of his ancestors' ghosts' intrusions into her mind. How could she ever share such a thing? Not only was he her boss, not her friend, but she'd found it difficult enough to share such things with Kirk.

She threw Jordan a glance. He stood a few feet away, swaying to the music with the rest of the crowd. He was tall and handsome, with fashionably mussed hair and tailored clothes made to look like he'd bought them from a thrift store. He had his arms around his current squeeze, Fae, a short, ornery hipster who had expertly put together his last-minute Halloween party. *Can't believe he wanted to come.* Katherine had mentioned off-hand that Kirk and his newly rechristened band had a gig and Jordan had insisted on getting tickets. Comped tickets, but tickets nonetheless. His insistence had thrown her as, outside of their business relationship, he'd shown zero interest in her personal affairs.

Jordan nodded to her his approval of Rodekill. His expression seemed to say "Can't believe they're actually kinda decent!"

## AUGUSTINE PIERCE

Fae was stone-faced. Katherine didn't know whether she was always like this, genuinely not liking much of anything, or whether that was all part of her professional persona—having to coolly dismiss everything that didn't quite fit in with her ultra-hip tastes.

Ultimately, Katherine didn't care what either Jordan or Fae thought of Kirk's band. She was here to have fun, a drink or two, and then curl up next to him when they got back to his place.

She'd begun staying with him because weeks ago, with her investigations into the mansion's mysteries, she'd discovered a unique piece of... it wasn't exactly jewelry, but it wasn't exactly anything else. She'd called it a pendant. It was the size of her palm and composed of five black metal bars fashioned in the shape of a V intersecting an equilateral triangle, with an in-laid stripe of platinum.

Since finding the pendant in a hidden study in the back of the mansion, the spirit of Vernon, Jordan's many-times-great grandfather, had haunted her, from appearing at King's Lanes bowling alley during a date with Kirk, to her usual eatery, the one diner in downtown Blackstone. The latter had been the most embarrassing as she'd totally lost it on a regular customer, thinking he was Vernon's ghost.

She hadn't shown her face since.

# THE FALL OF BLACKSTONE MANSION

Returning her gaze to Kirk, she felt a prick of guilt for having imposed on him, given she'd pre-paid six months' worth of rent at her own place. She wondered if it was time to wean herself off his, get back to staying at hers.

Kirk drilled into a very impressive, minute-long solo.

Katherine cheered some more. "Rock it!" *A little better than "Beam me up." A little.*

Kirk rattled those sticks across those drum heads like a possessed demon.

Katherine felt a tap on her shoulder.

Jordan again nodded his approval. "He's tight!"

"I know!" Katherine said.

"Don't say 'tight,'" Fae complained to Jordan.

"Why not?"

Fae cocked an eyebrow.

"Ah, come on," Jordan said. "I'm cool enough to pull off 'tight.'"

Fae shook her head, reached back around his waist, and squeezed his butt.

*Think I'm gonna hurl*, Katherine thought as she eagerly threw her attention back onto her sexy man. While she had zero problem with Jordan and Fae's relationship—if the trust-fund baby and the über-hipster wanted to drive each other nuts on a daily basis, that was their business—she had no desire to know any more details.

"Thanks for comin' out, everyone!" Rodekill's lead singer declared.

With that, the set concluded. The tiny crowd offered a smattering of applause and the band got to packing up.

"Wanna meet the band?" Jordan asked Fae.

"Um..." Fae sounded like she absolutely did not want to do so.

Jordan walked up to the lead singer and introduced himself and Fae. Katherine didn't hear the conversation, but it looked like the lead singer was at least being polite, shaking hands and smiling.

She sashayed over to Kirk. "That was really hot, baby."

He grinned bashfully. One of the things she loved about him was how unaware he was of his good looks. "Yeah?"

She leaned over next to his ear. "Kinda wanna ride you right here." She licked his earlobe.

He looked away, his grin spreading into a broad smile. "Um..." He nodded at his band mates, who were nearly finished packing up, and also in the middle of dealing with Jordan.

She stood up and switched her tone to more businesslike. "Could go to the bathroom. Take me in the stall."

Kirk looked concerned, as if she were being serious. "Um...?"

# THE FALL OF BLACKSTONE MANSION

She leaned over again. "Don't worry. I can wait till we get home."

He laughed, sounding very relieved, and continued packing up.

"You guys ready?" Jordan asked Katherine and Kirk.

"Sorry?" *Show's over, dude. We're goin' home. I've got some pent-up aggression to release on this boy!*

"Getting drinks with the band," Fae filled her in.

"With *this* band?" Katherine knew it was a stupid question, but she couldn't believe that Jordan and Fae were acting as if she and Kirk were going to spend the rest of their Friday night with them. *Are you that surprised, Kat?*

Fae gave Katherine a look that said "Yes, you pathetic excuse for a moron."

"Actually, guys, my kid's got soccer tomorrow," the lead singer informed them.

The two other members jumped right on his excuse with dazzling ones of their own.

*Lucky bastards*. She should have had an excuse locked and loaded and she didn't and now she and Kirk were going to have to spend who knew how many hours putting up with Jordan and Fae. Plus, even with as little as Katherine knew Fae, she knew the woman was not one to indulge even the slightest amount of time or attention in anything that even mildly annoyed her.

## AUGUSTINE PIERCE

"Well, looks like it's just us!" Jordan updated Katherine, as if she hadn't been standing a whole foot away.

"Yeah, I..." Katherine started.

Jordan's expression twisted from cheerful anticipation to stern expectation.

*He's not asking, Kat.*

"I'm down!" Kirk nodded. "Just another minute with this." He held up a stick and a cymbal.

"Great! This place, Oak Bar, is right down the street. Four and a half stars!" Jordan held up his phone to show off the Yelp listing.

"Love it!" Fae weighed in.

*Well, I guess destroying the bed will have to wait.*

Outside, they started in on their minute-long walk to the bar.

"Ooh," Jordan exclaimed while reading from his phone. "Check out these pics! They really do it up with the motif!" He held out his phone to show the others.

The group paused. Fae and Kirk leaned in for a closer look and both uttered polite responses. Katherine didn't feel like engaging. She felt like getting this next stop over with as soon as possible.

Flapping black.

Across the street. Peeking around the corner. The cloth resembled the edge of a flag a pirate captain would run up a pole. Except, as Katherine's eyes slowly traced its height, she found it was far taller than a mere flag. The next instant, she saw it. The edge of that pallid face she'd seen in downtown Blackstone and at the Halloween party. Ageless skin. Impossibly dark sunglasses. That wide-brimmed hat.

"Oh my God." She hurried across the street, not even bothering to watch for traffic.

"Kat, be careful!" Kirk called.

"Where you going?" Jordan asked.

"I'm fine!" Katherine assured Kirk. She reached the corner and stepped around it, ready to pounce on the man like a starving cat on the hunt.

The alley was empty.

"What is it?" Jordan sounded genuinely concerned, a first for him.

"Nothing," Katherine said.

## 2

*He's still watching me,* Katherine thought, regarding the man in black, whom she was sure she'd seen only seconds ago. *But why? He already knows everything about me. What else is there to learn?*

She, Kirk, Jordan, and Fae sat around a small table crafted from a slice of an oak trunk. That was the very literal theme of the Oak Bar, a quiet place with its tables, chairs, the bar, and wall panels all made from the wood.

Katherine, Kirk, and Fae sipped on beers and cocktails while Jordan monologued. While not paying attention to him, Katherine was pretty sure that he was still raving about the giant success that his Halloween party had been.

"Man, it was killer! Killer!" Jordan exclaimed.

"Congratulations," Kirk said.

"How many, Fae? Five hundred?"

"Don't have it in front of me. Over a thousand."

"She did such a great job!" Jordan squeezed her.

# THE FALL OF BLACKSTONE MANSION

She looked like she did not appreciate the gesture. She, in fact, looked like she was more eager to get out of here and go home than Katherine was.

"Too bad about your episode, Kat," Jordan said.

Hearing her name, Katherine finally paid attention. "What? Sorry? I was, uh..."

"Collapsing at the mansion after the lights went out," Jordan reminded her. "How long did the hospital keep you?"

"A few days," Kirk said.

Katherine felt he was really saying "She needed more, but you're such a jerk, you insisted she get back to work."

"Oh, uh, yeah. Too bad." *Is he actually sorry about my ghost-induced hospital stay?*

"Yeah, people really loved your story," Jordan said. "Gonna have to have you back next year for another retelling!"

Katherine had told a group of twenty partygoers of her and Kirk's adventure of locating and uncovering the body of Eileen Byrne, whom over a century earlier brothers Marcus and Reginald, the latter her fiancé, had murdered. The story had a particularly creepy vibe as the location where Katherine had told it, the ground floor of the mansion's west tower, was the exact spot where they'd found Eileen's remains.

Katherine was about to cut Jordan's idea of another retelling off at the root, but Kirk jumped in. "Maybe Kat should give that a think."

*Thanks, baby.*

"Oh, you know what we should do?" Jordan asked Fae. "We should make Kat the centerpiece. Lighting and everything!"

"There was lighting," Kirk reminded Jordan.

"No, but, like, lighting! Full-on theatrical! Make her the star!"

Fae's brow furrowed, most likely with the question of whether she was supposed to be taking notes.

"Yeah, I'll, uh, give that a good think." Katherine nodded at Kirk, not wanting to commit to anything.

"Listen to me. I've been going on and on," Jordan said.

Both Fae and Kirk insisted he wasn't.

"So, Kirk," Jordan said.

"Jordan," Kirk replied.

"Dude, you were hot on those bongos!"

"Thanks. I had my moments."

"No, he's right, baby," Katherine said. "You were on fire."

"You were fire," Fae said.

"Who's your label?" Jordan asked.

"Um"—Kirk looked at Katherine as if she should jump in here—"we're kinda between labels."

"No," Jordan said with a confident staccato, as if he'd just discovered the Beatles. "Not Rodekill's. Your label."

"Um"—Kirk again looked at Katherine like he really needed a life preserver—"I'm kinda between labels."

"You should talk to my guys at ArtHouse," Jordan said.

"They're, like, one of *the* top EDM labels in the world," Fae informed Kirk.

"Oh. Yeah, I don't really do EDM. And isn't that all electronic, anyway? Hence the E?"

"That's what I thought." Katherine was now simply trying to keep up with the conversation.

"Not as a DJ." Jordan pointed both index fingers at himself. "As a session guy, or we could totally hook you up with one of their sister label's acts." He grinned at Fae for backup.

Fae nodded, probably seeing the greater vision. "He is fire."

"Um, I dunno, uh..." Kirk stammered. He looked at Katherine with pleading eyes that said "Kat, help me out here!"

"Give him your contact, Jordan," Katherine said.

"Oh, right! Of course! Phone?"

Kirk took out his phone and handed it over.

Jordan added his information and updated his own phone with Kirk's. "Man, I am slammed this week, but we should talk. Maybe next week? Week after? If you don't hear from me, gimme a ring. Seriously, dude, day or night. I'm always up. Kat knows."

Katherine nodded. "I do."

Jordan handed Kirk his phone. "We'll get you hooked up with ArtHouse, outta that... Where are you now?"

"Car rentals," Kirk said.

Jordan's face twisted up, most likely disgusted by such a plebeian profession. "'S cool, man, but this'll be better."

Katherine tried to steer the conversation away from Jordan, possibly embarrassing Kirk. "That's how we met."

"How's that?" Jordan asked.

"I sold her a car," Kirk said.

"I thought you rented," Fae said.

"We sell 'em too."

Katherine felt like the conversation was about to die, which she would have preferred, but she wasn't sure yet whether that was a good idea. She opened her mouth to ask Fae about herself.

"I forgot! Kat, you got any T-giving plans?" Jordan asked.

*God, no. Do not invite me over for dinner.* "Um, not quite."

# THE FALL OF BLACKSTONE MANSION

"Don't make any. Probably gonna need you for another mansion event."

"Flattered, Jordan, but I told you, I'm not an event planner." Katherine nodded at Fae.

Fae raised her hand. "I am! Even got my own company." She smiled at Jordan.

He remained nonplussed. "Oh, totally. You're my girl. For, like, the deets, but Kat here, she's the big-picture chick."

Fae pursed her lips more and more at each of his mentioning of less than stellar terms for women, but said nothing.

*No I'm not!* Katherine shook her head at Fae. *Trust me, I am* not *trying to take your turf.*

"Halloween party was totally her idea!" Jordan said.

"It really wasn't," Katherine tried to reassure Fae.

Fae looked like she was just about done with this evening. "JB?"

"Yeah?" Jordan looked like he was desperate to launch into another monologue.

Katherine decided to help her out. "I think it's about time to turn in."

"Really?" Fae looked relieved at Katherine's having taken the charge.

"The night's still young!" Jordan declared.

"Well, I'm a little older than you guys," Katherine said.

"Not by *that* much."

"Well, we have plans tomorrow." Katherine wrapped her arm around Kirk.

It was their first weekend in nearly two months free of packing up and moving antiques out of the mansion. It would have been another working weekend, except Kirk had negotiated with Jordan on Katherine's behalf during her hospital stay. By Monday, though, everything would resume, starting with her selling the antiques out of her downtown Blackstone storefront to her various exclusive contacts.

Kirk looked very confused at her mentioning of plans, but nodded.

"What are you kids up to?" Jordan asked.

Katherine and Kirk answered at the same time.

"Picnic," Kirk said.

"Museum," Katherine said. "Picnic at a museum."

"A picnic?" Jordan asked. "It's November."

Katherine and Kirk stared at each other.

"Uh..." Kirk said.

"Yeah..." Katherine said.

"Not *that* cold. Park Blocks are beautiful this time of year." Fae referred to Portland's multi-block downtown strip of green space.

Jordan threw her a nasty glance, likely not appreciating her contradicting him. "Which museum?"

# THE FALL OF BLACKSTONE MANSION

His eyes shone with an eagerness that suggested he was about to invite himself.

Katherine and Kirk again answered at once.

"History," Kirk said.

"Science," Katherine said. "We, uh, haven't quite decided."

Fae informed Jordan, "I'll get the check." She held out her hand.

Jordan took out his wallet and gave her a black card.

Katherine whipped out her wallet. *No, Fae, I do not wanna owe him!* "No, let us!"

Kirk also took out his wallet. "No, *us*."

Jordan placed his hands over their respective wallets. "Your money's no good here."

"You sure, man?" Kirk asked.

"Write-off." Jordan grinned.

"Sorry?"

"You discussed business," Fae filled Kirk in.

"But we invited you," Katherine said, even though that was not at all the case.

"Money no good." Jordan nodded at Fae as if she were a servant off to do his bidding.

Fae didn't seem to mind as she smiled and walked over to the bar.

Katherine eased Kirk toward the exit. "Thank you guys so much for coming out and supporting my man."

"Yeah, thanks!" Kirk said.

Fae returned and gave Jordan his card.

"Seriously, dude, let's talk," Jordan told Kirk.

"Yeah, I'd love to."

"Shall we?" Fae dragged Jordan toward the exit.

They left the building and headed toward their cars.

"So, Kat, seriously, Thanksgiving," Jordan said. "What you got for me?"

"Can we talk about this Monday or Tuesday, or Friday?"

"Oh, yeah! 'Course! Take the weekend to simmer on it."

*How about the month?* She reached her car. "Good night, you guys."

"'Night," Fae said.

Jordan waved.

"You know, I do own an events company," Fae reminded Jordan.

"Heard you the last five times." Jordan was clearly losing his patience.

Katherine and Kirk got in.

Nearly slamming her door, she stared out the windshield. "Thank God that's over."

"Wasn't that bad," he said.

"You're just saying that 'cause he's gonna make you the next..." She realized she couldn't name a single drummer.

# THE FALL OF BLACKSTONE MANSION

"Danny Carey?"

"Who's that?"

"Drummer for Tool?"

"Who's that?"

"Only one of *the* greatest hard rock bands of all time?"

She grinned as she put on her seat belt and started the car. "Let's get outta here."

"Way ahead of you."

# 3

Katherine and Kirk lay in bed, nestled into each other.

"How you doing?" he asked.

"Me?" She hadn't registered his question.

"Yeah, you."

"Okay, I guess."

"You haven't said much since the hospital about, well, the hospital."

"No. I guess not." *What can I say? That I'm sick of ghosts dragging me into visions of their final moments before being murdered?*

"I mean, you don't have to, if you don't want to. Just observing that you haven't."

"Yeah, I hear you. I haven't been avoiding it, if that's what you're asking."

"Didn't think you were."

"I guess I've been so focused, first on getting out of the hospital, then on your gig, and on finishing our job."

"Oh, it's *our* job now?"

# THE FALL OF BLACKSTONE MANSION

"'Course it is!"

"Kat, I'm kidding."

"Oh, sorry."

"No more visits?"

"From... spirits?"

He nodded.

"No," she said. "Strangely, not at all."

"Isn't that a good thing? No more totaled cars?"

A recent occasion on which she was driving up to the mansion, Vernon's ghost had appeared in her back seat, causing her to slam into a tree. She'd totaled her car, but luckily, she'd made it through with only a few bruises.

"Yeah, it's just I'm suspicious," she said. "Unlike with Eileen, I didn't, ya know, resolve anything for them, so why haven't they kept pestering me?"

"Maybe all they wanted was for someone to know what happened."

In each of the Blackstone ghosts' visions, they'd shown Katherine how all three of their deaths had been at the hands of Marcus.

"Maybe, but it doesn't feel done," she said. "It feels like the eye of the storm."

"What about the man in black?"

She didn't want to report on earlier tonight, didn't want to get into it. So she told him something that was true. "Can't stop looking over my shoulder

everywhere I go, just in case he might be leering."
*From right across the friggin' street!*

Besides the man following her around, she suspected that he'd been behind a bouquet of black roses sent to her hospital room. The bouquet had included a cryptic poem, a take on *Jack and Jill*, that had recollected the car crash which she'd survived, but in which she'd lost her lifelong friend, Dean. The poem had even included a detail on how guilty she'd felt over his death. A detail she'd told no one.

The poem and the roses informed her that whoever sent them knew everything about her and could come after her at any time. Tonight was solid proof of that.

"That mean you're gonna keep investigating?" Kirk asked. "The mansion's tombs, those silver connectors you told me about?"

Below the mansion, there lay four tombs, one for each murdered family member and a final one for Eileen. Silver bands embedded into the floors connected each victim's concrete coffin to somewhere beyond the tombs, even deeper within the house.

"I dunno," she said. "I mean, you were right about their murderer, Marcus, dying decades ago. So, what else is there?"

"Don't forget that creepy pendant."

"I haven't." *I can't. I always need it near me. Always.*

# THE FALL OF BLACKSTONE MANSION

"Well, seems to me you still wanna know. Even if Marcus has been dead forever. One of the things I adore about you. You have to know."

"Adore?" She looked up at him and smiled.

They kissed.

"So, did he ever recover the bodies?" he asked.

After having discovered Gloria's body, Katherine had reported it to the police. They'd removed the remains and launched an investigation. But with her subsequent discovery of Reginald and Vernon's corpses, she'd reported them to Jordan, who had strangely insisted on not having them recovered. The Halloween party had raged over the dead.

Despite Kirk's insistence then and now, she hadn't followed up.

*God, Kirk, why can't you forget about that?* "I dunno."

"You never found out?"

"I was in the hospital."

"Well, right, but, Kat, I mean..."

She sat up. "No, you're right. Still a crime scene."

"And we were both there. Which makes us both—"

"I know. I know. I'll bring it up with him."

"Might wanna do it soon, 'cause..."

"I know."

They were quiet for a brief second.

"So, you think he's serious?" He was most likely trying to steer the conversation away from potential felonies.

"Jordan?" She lay down again and wrapped his arm around her.

"Yeah. About me becoming a 'session guy.'"

"I dunno. Maybe. Probably."

"You don't sound convinced."

"You've seen how he behaves. He gets an idea in his head, gets all engrossed in it, passionate about it, until the next shiny one comes along, and then it's all about that."

"Yeah."

"I'd just... I'd be careful to temper my expectations."

"Okay."

"He may do something for you or he may totally forget he ever mentioned it."

"Right."

She looked up at him. "That's not a reflection on you, cutie."

He grinned and nodded. "No, I know."

She kissed him again and nuzzled into his chest. They said nothing else and passed out in each other's arms.

The next day, Katherine and Kirk did not go to a museum or have a picnic. They slept in for half the day, except for the moment she'd shot up in bed at about 7:30, anticipating a call from Jordan. She hadn't realized how exhausting she'd found the previous evening until she and Kirk had gotten back.

She got up and checked the time. Twelve thirty-three. She gazed down at him. He was still fast asleep. She put on her underwear and went to the bathroom. After finishing, she stood in the hallway unsure whether she wanted to go back to bed or...

She snuck into the living room and sat on the couch. She eagerly reached into her purse. She felt like she was a drunk sneaking a swig, even peering down the hallway to make sure he wasn't coming.

Her hungry fingers wrapped around the pendant. She took it out and held it up to the afternoon light coming in through the windows. She'd never ceased to be amazed at how the piece's unidentified black metal reflected no light and yet its platinum vein gleamed so brightly.

She held it in her left hand as she ran her right index finger around its triangle and V again and again. She thought about Kirk's questions last night. About whether she'd keep up her attempts to unravel the mansion's mysteries. *I do wanna know more about you*, she thought, regarding the pendant. *Need to know.* It no longer surprised her that she thought of the piece as a long-distance lover with whom she was about to passionately reunite. It no longer bothered her that she thought about it every moment of every day.

# AUGUSTINE PIERCE

"Hey," Kirk said.

She shouted. The pendant dropped onto her lap, then to the floor. "Don't *do* that!"

"Sorry. Thought you heard me come in."

She shot to her feet. "Well, I didn't!" She bent over and picked up the pendant. "Look what you made me do!"

"Sorry, Kat, I really thought you heard me."

She turned the pendant over and over in her hands, searching for any scratches, but found none.

"It's probably gonna be okay." He grinned.

"You don't know that!"

"What's it made of? Steel?"

"I don't know! Probably zirconium. Doesn't matter. You can't just sneak up on me like that!"

He attempted to embrace her. "Hey, Kat, I'm sorry. I really didn't mean to—"

"Don't touch me." She sounded far more insistent than she intended.

He stepped back and looked away. "Did I do something?"

"No."

"Then why are you so upset?"

"I'm not."

"Yes, you are. You just told me not to touch you after I accidentally startled you."

She said nothing.

# THE FALL OF BLACKSTONE MANSION

"Look, you wanna get some breakfast?" he asked. "There's a nice place nearby I've been meaning to try."

She headed for the bedroom. "I think I should just go."

"Kat?"

She ignored him as she got dressed and threw her things into her carry-on.

"I'm sorry I startled you," he said. "I didn't mean to. Let's forget it and get some breakfast."

"I'll call you later."

"Where are you going?"

"My place."

"But I gave you a key because..."

"I'll be fine." She exited and slammed the door shut behind her.

She floored it on her way back to her own apartment. *Why are you being such a bitch to Kirk?* "I don't know," she told her reflection in the rearview as she wiped tears from her eyes. She knew he didn't mean to startle her. She knew he was offering an olive branch with his suggestion of breakfast. *Why did I push him away?* "I'll call him later and apologize. I'll tell him it was left over from Jordan pissing me off." *Better come up with a better reason than that.* "Like what?" she asked herself.

She half expected to see Vernon's ghost there again, waiting for her, but the back seat was empty.

On entering her unit, she halted in the doorway. She'd only been here once since her release from the hospital, and that time was with Kirk. While she didn't expect to encounter any spirits, she could never be sure.

*This is why you shouldn't have picked a fight.* "I know. I'll apologize." She took a deep breath. "All right, spirits. I'm comin' in and I'm not in the mood. So let's keep the jump scares to a minimum, hm?"

The living room didn't answer.

She took three steps in and paused again. She listened, but heard nothing. She rubbed the back of her neck, but felt nothing there either. "'Kay, I'm gonna assume you'll at least let me take stuff off."

No reply from the apartment.

She exhaled sharply, closed the door behind her, and walked in the rest of the way. Standing right next to the end of her sofa, she took off her purse and set it on the arm. While she was certain that the pendant contained within had been the gateway through which Vernon's spirit had reached out, or in the very least had aided in its contact, she still couldn't bring herself to handle the item in any other way than the most careful and respectful.

She removed her jacket and lay it on top of her purse. Still suspecting a ghost's possible arrival, she looked around at the empty living room. Satisfied nothing was going to happen, she gave the space a convinced nod.

She wheeled her carry-on into her bedroom and unpacked her laptop. While she didn't know that Kirk would welcome her back after an apology, she hoped he would, so chose not to unpack any clothes or toiletries.

Taking her laptop to the bed, she lay down and opened it. She stared at the screen. *I should call him.* She turned on the computer. *No, I should give him some time.* She opened the browser and stared at its blankness. *If I call him to apologize and ask him if I can still stay, he'll think I only called to make sure I can stay.* She kept staring at that browser window. *Crap, Kat, you still gotta work with the guy. Can't act like this if you expect that to run smoothly. Setting aside you're being a jerk to your boyfriend.* "I'll call him in a sec."

She went to her e-mail, opened a draft message, and started typing a list. "One, the man in black. Who is he?" She searched for that simple phrase "man in black," but the first result was about the famous sci-fi comedy film franchise *Men in Black*. She understood why that was the top result, but it frustrated her that she'd have to dig. And dig. She tried various combinations of terms like "long, black trench coat" and "wide-brimmed hat," but nothing came close to an image of the man she'd seen. For now, this search was futile.

"Two, Miles and Nigel couldn't help with the pendant, so..."

Miles, her British friend who also dealt in antiques, had recommended her to his acquaintance, Nigel, an expert in esoteric symbolism, but other than informing her that the pendant was in the shape of a rare occult symbol, he couldn't help her with anything further. Nor could a metallurgist with the type of metal that composed the piece, nor a jeweler with the shape of the symbol in which it was fashioned and the platinum vein that ran through it.

"Three, the county records lady couldn't give me any info on the mansion's floor plan, so gotta figure something else out."

After she'd realized that the shape of the pendant—the symbol it represented—and the mansion's floor plan were identical, and given what she already knew about the tombs' silver bands likely connecting beneath the house, she knew there must have been some part of the plan she hadn't yet seen. She'd assumed someone had included it in some official record.

"Four, Marcus, what happened to him?" She placed her hands on her lap. "Just call him."

She dug her phone out of her pants pocket, held it up, and hesitated. She goaded herself in a sing-song voice. "Call him."

She tapped Kirk's number. He picked up.

# THE FALL OF BLACKSTONE MANSION

"Hey." Concern filled his voice.

*Phew! He's not pissed. Looks like I was the only one who was.* "Hey, listen, I'm really—"

"It's okay, Kat. Let's just talk, or if you don't wanna, I can listen."

"No, it's not okay. I was mean, and I didn't have a good reason to be."

"I wouldn't say 'mean,' exactly."

"I dunno what's goin' on, Kirk. Ever since I moved here, ever since I first walked into that damn mansion. Ever since I found the pendant..."

"Maybe you should put it back in that dusty study."

*Maybe you should shove it up your—! Whoa, Kat! This is what he was talking about! What gives?* "Um, maybe..." *Or maybe not.* "Listen, I'm doing some research, maybe for an hour, maybe more, but after that... I don't want you to think that I'm only calling for this 'cause I did owe you an apology, but I can still stay with you, right?"

She could hear that he was grinning. He dragged the syllables out and chuckled. "I dunno... Of course you can stay. One little skirmish isn't gonna stop that."

"Skirmish?"

"Seemed like a good word for it."

"Thanks."

"Of course, Kat. Listen, maybe depending on when you drop by, we can get dinner."

"I'd like that."

"Then who knows? Maybe tomorrow we can do that museum-picnic combo."

"Even though it's the dead of November?"

He laughed. "Right?"

"Yeah, sounds nice."

"I'll let you get to your research."

"Thanks. You're a sweetheart."

"See you soon."

"Bye." She hung up and set her phone on the bedside table. *He's too good to me.*

She looked back at her list. "Marcus." She clicked over to the browser and typed in his name. Quite a few results popped up. Among them, she saw no mention of any criminal activity. "Makes sense. He got away with murdering his whole family and Eileen." Katherine found he died in 1999 at the ripe old age of ninety-six. He'd been living in some other mansion in northwest Portland. It was neither as big nor ostentatious as the one tucked away in Mt. Hood's foothills. From the looks of it, he'd spent his life as a very private beneficiary of his family's estate. There seemed to be no evidence of a frolicking, playboy lifestyle like that of his descendant, Jordan. Marcus had married at thirty-five to a Cecilia Caldwell, herself the heiress to a mining fortune Katherine had never heard of. They'd had three children, one who was also one of Jordan's ancestors. There was little intriguing information beyond that.

"So he murders his family, marries some other rich jerkoff, and chills? That's it?" It crossed her mind that Marcus may have continued in his hobby of knocking off family members, but not only did she doubt that, there was no evidence. "Could've covered it up again. Paid off police or whatever." No, that didn't feel right. Marcus's crimes against his family of origin felt like a singularity. He'd had a purpose for that and once he'd fulfilled that purpose... He didn't read as a serial killer. "The Realm. The Formula." Those were among Marcus's parting words to his dying brother, Reginald. "What did he mean by those, and how would I find out?"

She had no idea. Absolutely none. She could ask Jordan, but not only did she suspect he also had no idea, but even if he did, why would he tell her? Besides, how would that conversation even go? *Hey, Jordan, so your great-whatever grandfather, what did he mean, in the vision his dead brother's ghost gave me, by "the Realm" and "the Formula"? Oh, you have no idea? Thanks!*

As much as she hated to admit it, the fact was she had to keep looking at the mansion. Thankfully, she had good reason to return, what with so many rooms left to pack up and sell off. But what to look for and where to start?

## AUGUSTINE PIERCE

She dinked around on her computer for another hour before she threw her laptop in her carry-on and headed back to Kirk's place.

4

"How married are you to Creek?" Katherine asked.

"Married?" Kirk asked.

They sat on a blanket in Creek's downtown park blocks, enjoying a picnic of bread, cheese, salami, jam, and white wine on this beautiful Sunday afternoon. While it was a touch on the chilly side, they'd both felt the need to have this picnic to spite Jordan's scoffing at the idea of it.

*Great, Kat. Now he thinks you're fishing for a proposal after, what, two weeks of official dating?* "Yeah. Living here." *Should I clarify I'm not looking for a proposal?*

"Um, I mean, not married. Not at all. Only here 'cause of the job, which I told you I'm not so sure about either."

"I remember."

"Why do you ask?"

"Well..." She flipped a slice of salami around her fingers, unsure of how to continue, then gobbled it up. "We'll be done with the mansion in not too long.

As much as I've enjoyed the peace, quiet, and beauty of rural Oregon, I'm gettin' kinda itchy."

"To move?"

"To move on."

He nodded.

"Maybe," she said.

"Where you thinking of going?"

"Haven't decided yet. Maybe San Francisco, LA."

"Big antique scenes in those places?"

"That's the thing. After all the craziness that's gone down with the mansion, I don't know that I'm even looking for a scene."

"But isn't that your work?"

"Yes," she said hesitantly.

"I'm no accountant, but what would you do for work?"

"I'd be good for a while. I have my savings from before working for Jordan, and after that's all done, I'll have more."

"So retire?"

"Take a break. Ride the cable car." She grinned at the idea of spending months doing nothing but riding San Francisco's signature form of public transportation.

"So after the first half hour?"

"Right? Before I came out here, I was part-time doing assessment for rich people on pieces they'd either bought or were thinking of buying. Ensuring authenticity."

"Uh-huh?"

"That's, in fact, what I was doing the day I flew out here."

"Gotcha."

"So after a little break, I might do that a bit more full-time."

"So cable car for half an hour, a trip to Alcatraz, then full-time... authentication?"

"Maybe."

"Sounds like a plan to me."

"So I wanna know... I know we're still early days, but, I mean, we're already kinda living together..."

"Sure."

"You don't know what I was gonna ask."

"If I wanted to join you in San Francisco or LA, where you'll authenticate antiques for rich people?"

She smiled wide. "Okay, that was what I was gonna ask."

"Yeah. Let's do it. One thing, though?"

"Yeah."

"What would I do?"

"I know you don't wanna keep handing car keys to tourists."

"Not exactly my favorite thing, no."

"I was thinking, what about doing what you love?"

"Drumming?"

"Why not?"

"You don't apply for that."

"You don't think you could find a band in need in LA?"

"Finding a band in need isn't really the issue."

"Okay."

"It's finding an employed band in need."

"Right."

"Technically, that's what I'm doing now, but like I told you and the guys weeks ago, hard to pay the bills."

"What if you didn't have to pay the bills?" She regretted how eager she sounded.

"What do you mean?"

"What if part of the arrangement was that you don't have to worry about that? For a while?"

"You mean you pay for everything?"

"I mean, not *everything* and not forever. Just, while I'm breaking and then authenticating, you look around, see if you can find a band to join. We play that by ear—pardon the pun—for, I dunno, six months, then reassess. Worst thing that can happen is you have to go back to handing car keys to tourists, and in this little adventure, your ability to eat wouldn't rely solely on doing that."

"I like that."

"What?"

"Little adventure."

"So do I."

"So let me see if I understand."

"Uh-huh?"

"We—you and I—we move to San Francisco or LA."

"Or somewhere else."

"We get a place together."

"Kinda like now."

"We ride the cable car."

"Every day."

"You chill, then authenticate."

"Uh-huh."

"I look for drumming gigs."

"That's right."

"Failing that, I go back to whatever."

"If you want to, yeah."

"But otherwise, you pay for stuff?" He sounded very suspicious.

"I wouldn't have to, of course. I'm just saying you wouldn't be under intense pressure to hand quite so many keys out to quite so many tourists."

"Can I think about it?"

"Yeah. Of course."

"It's just I've been at the rental place a while and to take off..."

"Afraid of missing Annie?" She referred to his coworker whom she'd accused of being in love with him.

He shrugged. "I dunno. A little."

Her phone *buzzed* in her pocket. "Who could this be?"

"You get a thousand guesses, but the first nine hundred and ninety-nine don't count." He grinned.

She took out her phone. It was Jordan. She sighed. "I don't wanna."

"You should," Kirk said.

"But it's a Sunday and I don't wanna."

"As I recall, neither of those factors ever mattered to him."

"You're right." She struggled to stand. "'Scuse me."

"Go get 'im."

"Be right back."

He smiled. "Take your time."

She walked several feet away and answered. "Happy Sunday, Jordan." She emphasized the day to let him know she did not want to talk.

"Kat! Happy Sunday!"

"We're actually in the middle of a picnic—"

"So, when are you and your team getting back to it?"

"Well, since I'm out of the hospital"—she emphasized the word hospital—"we can start as soon as this weekend."

"Today?" He sounded so excited.

"No, this coming weekend. As in next Saturday."

"Oh."

# THE FALL OF BLACKSTONE MANSION

"As previously agreed."

"Right. Okay."

"So, uh, I'm gonna go ahead and—"

"Thanksgiving."

"Yeah?" *You want me to plan the whole thing for you?*

"I'm thinking we invite a bunch of foodies, influencers, etc."

*We?*

"Hire a top-shelf restaurant to cater," he continued.

"Uh-huh?"

"Put the restaurant in the kitchen, have 'em use the actual stuff in there, like, the old pots and pans."

"Okay."

"It'll be an authentic, opulent Thanksgiving like my great-grandparents enjoyed."

"All right."

"What do you think?"

"Sounds like a plan, though…"

"Uh-huh?"

"You think there'll be much demand for that sort of thing?"

"I think if we have influencers, there will be."

"Is there room?"

"What do you mean?"

"Dining room's not that big."

"Ah, that's where VIP status comes in."

"You lost me."

"We have the influencers and VIPs in the dining room, everyone else at set up tables and chairs in, like, the entryway hall."

"So, ten VIPs in the dining room."

"Yeah."

"Everyone else everywhere else."

"Yeah."

"If you think you can throw it together."

"I'll have Fae take care of that."

"Guess you don't need me."

"Ah, but I do."

"For what?"

"I need you and your team not to move any of the dining room or kitchen stuff. And actually, none of the stuff in surrounding rooms."

"Okay."

"To keep the authentic feel."

"Gotcha." She wasn't sure if she should ask her next question. "Were you gonna spin again?"

He paused for several seconds. "You think I should?"

"I don't know that dance music would lend itself to a serene, opulent Thanksgiving dinner."

"You're right. You're right! I'll have Fae bring in some harpists or something."

"Well, sounds like you've got it all figured out, so I'll get back to my picnic with Kirk—"

"What do you think of her?"

"Who?" *Jordan, why are you asking me? We're not friggin' friends! You threatened to sue me only a few weeks ago!*

"Fae."

*Crap. What do I say? If he likes her, I can't rag on her. If he doesn't, I should.* "Fae's a consummate professional."

"She's *very* professional. After we got back last night? From Kirk's show?"

"Yeah?"

He whistled. "Between you and me? Fae is a *demon* in the sack."

"Um..." Katherine eyed Kirk.

He raised his glass of wine and took a sip.

"Why I called so late today," Jordan continued. "Li'l fox kept me up all night and woke me up for more this morning."

"Yeah, Jordan, I dunno that this is any of my business."

"Oops. Sorry. Too much?"

"A little."

"Don't sue me for sexual harassment, okay?" He laughed.

"Wouldn't dream of it."

"J, you comin' back?" Fae asked in Jordan's background.

"Yeah, one sec," Jordan replied. "So, yeah, don't move anything around the kitchen or dining room," he repeated to Katherine.

*Crap. If I don't ask him about the bodies, Kirk'll keep bugging me.* "Wouldn't dream of that either."

"Oh, and tell Kirk I haven't forgotten him."

"Sorry?" The need to interject about the bodies was distracting her.

"His drumming. My label."

"I'll pass that along. Hey, Jordan? I need to ask you something."

"Jay Bee!" Fae faux whined.

"Better go. Duty calls," Jordan informed Katherine.

"Again, don't need to know," Katherine said. "Jordan, the bodies."

"The what?"

"The corpses of your great-grandfather and uncle. You ever recover them? It was over a hundred years ago, but still a crime."

"Yeah, don't worry about that."

"Don't worry? Did you call the police and recover them or not?"

His tone fell deadly serious. "I'm telling you not to worry."

She marched a few more feet from Kirk so he wouldn't hear the profound concern in her voice. "What're you doing? Those are human remains.

# THE FALL OF BLACKSTONE MANSION

They were murdered. They deserve a proper burial—"

His tone remained serious. "I'll talk to you soon." He hung up.

She stared at her phone a second before putting it back in her pocket and returning to Kirk.

"What was that all about?" he asked.

She paused before sitting, still struck by Jordan's reaction. "Jordan stuff."

"Heard you mention the bodies you found."

She picked up another slice of salami, but didn't eat it, instead holding it in front of her mouth. "I don't think he's had them recovered."

"Then we need to call the police."

"No." She squeezed his arm. "At least not yet."

"Why?"

"I don't know what he could do me—to us—legally."

Kirk nodded, but still looked very troubled by the whole situation. She munched the salami slice.

"I can't shake this feeling that something's coming down the pike," she said.

"Something worse than us being accomplices to a disturbingly twisted crime?"

She shook her head. "No clue. And that's what scares me."

5

Katherine was already half awake, squeezing Kirk's hand as he spooned her. She was thinking about their previous day's picnic, Jordan's rude interruption, and the dinner that she and Kirk had shared a few hours later to cleanse her palette of Jordan's call.

*Buzz!* Her phone vibrated on the nightstand.

"Mm..." The half asleep part of her mind was still waking up.

"Probably Jordan," Kirk mumbled.

"Probably gonna berate me or fire me over bringing up his stupid, dead family." She eased out of Kirk's embrace, sat up, and checked her phone. *Yep. And at eight on the dot. He really does never sleep.*

She stumbled out to the living room and answered. "'Morning, Jordan."

"Kat! What are you up to today?" He sounded shockingly cheerful, considering how their last conversation had ended.

"Selling your stuff."

# THE FALL OF BLACKSTONE MANSION

"That's today?"

"It's Monday and I'm back on the clock."

"What time are you doing that?"

"Afternoon. Why?"

"Perfect! I need you to come out here."

"Your place? Portland?"

"Yeah."

"Why? I'm just gonna have to drive all the way back out here."

"We need to meet."

"Can it wait till I'm done?"

"Nope."

"You sure?"

"Try to be here by nine thirty."

She turned the phone away so he wouldn't hear her sigh. "Okay, then I'd better go since it's about an hour and some change to get out there."

"See you soon." He hung up.

She marched back to the bedroom and plugged in her phone.

"That him?" Kirk asked.

"Yeah. I'm gonna take a shower and go."

"That urgent, huh?"

"I dunno. Probably needs me to rescue his cat from a tree."

He chuckled. "Right?"

"See you tonight." She bent over him and kissed his cheek.

"See ya."

She took a quick shower and got going. She had to drive fast to make it to Jordan's condo in northwest Portland's trendy Pearl District by nine thirty. She made it to the area with ten minutes to spare. She parked and stomped to his building, the Vista, the tallest skyscraper in the area.

She tapped his name on the directory. He didn't answer, rather buzzed her in. Entering the elevator, she wiped the remaining sleep from her eyes. While she wasn't concerned with presenting herself professionally, she didn't want to invite any irritating questions like "Late night?" or "You and Kirk get down to it?" or whatever else Jordan's inappropriate mind might dream up. Reaching his door, which surprisingly wasn't vibrating with his usual dance music, she knocked.

Hurried footsteps arrived at the other side. "Here she is!" Jordan sounded like he was announcing to someone else.

*Great. Is Fae here? Wouldn't surprise me. Ever since they started, she's been hanging around.*

Jordan opened the door. "Kat! 'Morning!"

"Hey, Jordan. What's going on?"

He held the door open for her. She stepped in. It was an upscale space with a glorious view of the city and river, and a sunken living area with couches and a glass-shard firepit. She couldn't help but let her eyes feast on that view. It stole her attention each time she'd been here.

"Sushi?" Jordan asked.

"For breakfast?" Katherine asked.

"Why not?" a young-sounding female voice asked from the sunken area.

*That's not Fae. Sounds too young and happy.*

She turned to find a pretty blonde, late twenties, sitting on the couch nearest the window. She wore a gray turtleneck sweater and jeans. Her clothes weren't designer like Jordan's always were, so Katherine doubted she was a friend, at least not a close one. But the woman didn't look like he'd brought her in from off the street. She put a piece of sashimi in her mouth and chewed hungrily.

"'Morning." Katherine approached the woman with her hand extended.

"Ah, crap! My manners!" Jordan met both women at the top of the sunken area's stairs. "Kat—Katherine Norrington—this is Stacey Webber. Stacey, this is my associate, Kat."

Stacey wiped her hands and stood. She and Katherine shook hands. "Everybody calls me C. So nice to meet you. J's told me all about you."

"Nice to meet you too, C. Afraid I can't say the same," Katherine said. *Who is this chick and why am I here? Oh no, is she some Fae-alternate? He's not gonna tell me about sex with this woman too, is he?*

"Stacey is my fourth cousin," Jordan said with pride.

*Fantastic, Jordan. Why did I drag my ass all the way out here?*

"Fifth," Stacey corrected.

"Right! Keep forgetting that!" Jordan said.

"Great! Very cool." Katherine had no clue what else to say, but figured she'd at least play along.

"You know those family-DNA sites?" Jordan asked Katherine.

"I'm familiar."

"I jump on one, order the kit, swab the cheek, couple weeks later get all this crazy info, like, my family's mostly from England."

"With a name like Blackstone?" Katherine knew her sarcasm might rub them the wrong way, but she didn't care. She didn't want to be here and wasn't ashamed to let them know it.

"Exactly! Anyway, who shows up in my recommendations?"

"Ta-da!" Stacey smiled.

*He's awfully excited about some long-lost cousin when he can't even be bothered to look at his mansion that's pulling in millions.*

"And she lives right here in town!" Jordan said.

"Actually, I'm pretty close to Gresham." Stacey referred to the suburb east of Portland.

"Eh, close enough."

# THE FALL OF BLACKSTONE MANSION

"Join us?" Stacey sat down and gestured for Katherine to do the same.

"Sure." Katherine sat next to her. She noticed that in anticipation of her arrival, Jordan had ordered a plate of sushi for her. Among the selections were yellow tail and red snapper. *Huh. He remembered.* She scooped up a piece of yellow tail.

Jordan sat on the perpendicular couch. "Small world. Crazy."

"Yeah!" Stacey said.

"So C does actual work."

"I try." Stacey waved it off.

"What do you do?" *And what am I doing here?*

"I work at a flower shop." Stacey nodded.

*Not curing cancer, but better than pretending to be a DJ.*

"Kat's in antiques," Jordan filled in Stacey. "Selling off all the old junk in the mansion."

*Huh. He said "the" mansion. Like he's mentioned it before. Guessing he's already given her all the gory details of his fortune.*

"That's so fascinating!" Stacey sounded genuinely interested. "So you just find old houses, assess their things, and sell 'em?"

Katherine nodded. "That pretty much sums it up."

"She's also fantastic at other stuff," Jordan bragged.

*Like what, Jordan? Where's this going?*

"Oh?" Stacey asked.

"That Halloween blowout I told you about? Totally Kat's idea," Jordan said.

"I dunno about that," Katherine said.

"Eh, she's being modest." Jordan gobbled up some tuna, barely covering his mouth while he chewed.

"So, um, Jordan, I appreciate the breakfast and meeting you, Stacey..." Katherine began.

"C," Stacey corrected.

"C. Sorry."

Stacey nodded and grinned.

"But why'd you call me up here?" Katherine asked.

"Right!" Jordan rubbed his palms together. He picked up a piece of paper next to the far side of the firepit that Katherine hadn't noticed and passed it to her. "Like I've said, I need an ideas person."

Katherine looked at the paper. It contained legal jargon, his name, and her name.

"That is an offer, an official one, for you to join the trust," Jordan explained.

Katherine regarded him curiously. "I'm sorry. I don't understand."

Jordan grinned like a little boy about to get on an exciting theme park ride. "I want you to be its director."

"What?" Katherine asked with complete incredulity.

"Told you she'd be shocked," Stacey opined.

# THE FALL OF BLACKSTONE MANSION

"You were right!" Jordan addressed Katherine. "You'll have direct access to my attorneys, won't have to get my go on anything. You can handle everything directly."

Katherine set the paper on the firepit. "I don't understand. Don't you already have people for this?"

Jordan shrugged. "Eh, I mean..."

"You know I don't have any executive experience."

Jordan waved that off.

"Or any experience in trusts or even banks," Katherine said.

"If she doesn't want it, I'll take it!" Stacey offered.

Jordan's good cheer vanished for a second as he shot her a nasty glance that said "Shut up, kid." "Look at the salary." He pointed at the paper.

Katherine picked it up again. She searched for a second, then found it. Two hundred and fifty thousand a year. *Damn. Is that in addition to my commission?*

"That's in addition to your percentage of selling the junk," Jordan confirmed.

Katherine set the paper down again and sank back into the couch. "Jordan..."

Jordan leaned forward. "You know Robert Evans?"

"No."

"Head of Paramount Pictures in the seventies?"

That rang a bell. Katherine had a vague memory of the notorious studio head who'd been plucked from obscurity to run the studio, and had led it to its most successful years up to that point. "I'm familiar."

"Picked *Chinatown*, *Rosemary's Baby*, all that?"

"Right?"

"Didn't know squat about running a studio!"

"What about Fae?" *If anyone should run anything for you, it should be someone who's already run something for you.*

Jordan waved off that suggestion too. "Fae's fantastic at details. But I told you, I need my ideas lady!" He eyed Stacey. "Besides, Fae and I are kinda, well..." He made the universal "we're screwing" gesture.

Katherine sat up. "Jordan! Stop! Please!"

Jordan dropped his hands and informed Stacey. "She's totally gonna sue me for harassment one of these days."

Stacey didn't sound all that amused. "Yeah, I bet."

Katherine picked up the offer letter. "Can I think about this?"

"Sure, but don't take too long," Jordan said. "I need ideas!"

Katherine stuffed the letter in her purse and stood. "I, uh, need to go."

Jordan and Stacey stood as well.

"Back to selling my stuff?" he asked Katherine.

"Yeah."

"Not gonna finish your sush?" Jordan pointed at Katherine's nearly full plate.

Katherine didn't answer him as she stepped past Stacey.

Stacey shrugged. "More for me."

Still feeling dumbfounded by all this, Katherine offered Stacey her hand. "Nice to, uh, meet you, C."

"Hope to see you again soon." Stacey accepted her hand.

"You two should exchange info," Jordan suggested, but then he waited for it to happen.

"Yeah, uh..." Katherine said.

She and Stacey took out their phones and exchanged numbers.

"Never before nine." Katherine grinned.

"That's when I call." Jordan laughed.

"Never after 2:00 a.m." Stacey smiled, attempting to join in on the banter.

"So, let me know how it goes." Jordan didn't offer Katherine his hand.

"Will do," Katherine said.

"And don't leave me hanging on the..." Jordan pointed to her purse.

"Yeah. I'll give it some thought." Katherine practically ran out of there.

6

"What's there to think about?" Kirk asked over the speakers in Katherine's car.

"What do you mean, what's there to think about?" Katherine asked.

"It's a good salary, right?"

"That's not the point!"

"What is the point?"

"I wanted to move once I was done with the mansion. If I accept this, I'll be at his beck and call even more than I am now."

"So then refuse it."

*You're not helping, Kirk!* "What would you do?"

He was quiet for a second. "God, I dunno. I mean, that's a lotta money, but you're right. He'd own you."

"More than he does now!" she reiterated. "That wasn't even the weirdest part."

"Oh?"

"He had some cousin there."

"Cousin?"

"Yeah, he found her on some DNA site."

"And she was just hanging with you guys?"
"Yup."
"Why?"
"I dunno! He's just like, 'Hey, this is my cousin.'"
"Weird."
"Yeah! Nothing makes sense! Nothing ever makes sense with this stupid family!"
"If you do take it, when do you have to tell him?"
"He didn't give me a specific deadline."
"Then I'd drag it out."
"Really?"
"Yeah, I mean, sounds like you don't want it, but I understand if you don't wanna tell him that right away, so drag it out."
"I love that, would love to torture him, but I should get back to him soon. He's not exactly patient."
"Have a lawyer look at it."
"Yeah. Make sure I'm not giving him my first-born."
"You have a first-born?" He sounded faux concerned.
"God no, but if I did..."
"Hey, I'm sorry, but..."
"No, I know. You're at work."
"Yeah. Good luck with today. See you tonight."
"See you. And Kirk?"
"Uh-huh?"

## AUGUSTINE PIERCE

"Thanks for talking."

She could hear him smile. "Any time," he said.

They hung up.

In another hour, she was back in Blackstone and pulling up to her store with the red awning. Today she was auctioning off the mansion's smoking room. She expected the process to go smoothly, but the last time she'd stepped foot inside, Vernon's ghost had contacted her, so she stayed in her car until anyone arrived.

She peered out both front windows, but saw no sign of the man in black. *Maybe I scared him off Friday. Yeah, doubt that, Kat. Gotta figure out a way to spy on him or track him down.* "But how?"

No longer wanting to think about him, she eyed her purse, at first pondering Jordan's offer, and then... *The pendant.* She knew she shouldn't. Every time she gazed at it, every time she touched it, she didn't want to stop. It was like her whiskey, if she were an alcoholic. The black-and-platinum trinket had started her fight with Kirk over the weekend and nearly cost her relationship with Aleeyah, her New York-based antiques contact, when Katherine had refused to sell her the piece after Aleeyah had caught sight of it in Katherine's purse.

*I shouldn't.* She held her hand over her purse, but pulled it back. The next thing she knew, she was unzipping it and shoving her hand inside. She took out the pendant and, just like an addict, felt immense relief as she held it up and ran her finger along its bars. *Never did figure you out.* Its origin and meaning, other than what Nigel had told her, were a complete mystery.

She held it up to the windshield and regarded the black metal. No highlights. No sparkles. No gleaming. Nothing at all. She thought back to one thing Nigel had told her. *"There are very fringe voices who say that the symbol originates not of this world... A realm beyond our reality."*

"That true?" she asked the pendant. "You from beyond our reality?"

*Knock knock knock!* Someone's knuckles rapped on her window.

"Crap!" She dropped the pendant. Panicking, she reached down to pick it up, but her fingers couldn't find it.

"Sorry! Didn't mean to startle you!" a young-sounding female voice said.

Katherine looked to her left. A petite, very attractive brunette in her mid twenties, wearing a smart suit, stood right next to her door. "Uh, that's fine. Just gimme a sec."

"Sure."

Katherine looked down. The pendant wasn't in her lap. With adrenaline surging, she searched the floor. *Where is it? Where is it? Where is it?*

Black and sparkling platinum.

She located the pendant right between her feet. *Thank God!* She picked it up.

"What's that?" Ms. Brunette asked.

"Nothing! Nothing, just a, uh..." Katherine shoved the piece back into her purse. She smiled at her. "Nothing." She rolled down her window.

"'Afternoon!" Ms. Brunette offered her hand.

"Uh, can I help you?" *She's too nicely dressed to be homeless.*

"I'm McKenzie. I work for Aleeyah Morgan?"

*Of course you're hot. Aleeyah'd* never *hire an actual mortal.*

"She sent me to check out the smoking room pieces," McKenzie explained.

*Leeyah didn't come herself and didn't tell me she was sending someone. Still pissed I didn't sell her the pendant. Probably also annoyed I kinda tried to steal her phone.* "Right! Of course! Sorry, McKenzie. How are you?"

"Is now a bad time?"

"No. No, no, no." Katherine shook her hand. "Sorry. A little distracted."

McKenzie stepped away from the door. "Not too early, am I?"

Katherine checked her phone. Seven past noon. "Nope. Right on time."

"Great. I'll be over here." McKenzie pointed to a luxury sedan.

# THE FALL OF BLACKSTONE MANSION

"Wonderful. Be right with you." Katherine rolled up her window, grabbed her purse, and got out.

Beyond McKenzie's rental, Katherine saw no other cars. "You the first?"

"Looks like it."

"Well, uh, thanks for coming."

"Yeah. Aleeyah sends her best. Sorry she couldn't make it."

"That's fine. I understand. New York keeps her pretty busy."

McKenzie shook her head. "You have no idea."

Katherine took out her store keys. "So, uh, shall we?"

"After you, Kat—Oh, can I call you Kat?"

"I prefer that, McKenzie."

"Eh, Kenzie's cool."

"All right. Let's go." Katherine unlocked the front door and held it open for her. Inside sat sofas, tables, chairs, ashtray stands, and other items from the mansion's smoking room.

"Wow! Aleeyah wasn't kidding! This stuff is amazing!"

"Yeah, it's pretty nice."

"Is it true?"

"What's that?"

"That the owner's great-great-whatever grandfather murdered his whole family?"

"It is."

"Crazy. Any idea why? They ever catch the prick?"

"No and no, unfortunately." Katherine didn't know why Marcus had murdered them, but suspected it had to do with the Formula and Realm. She knew they had something to do with the mansion and the pendant, as Marcus had been wearing it during the vision of the ghost of his father, Vernon, but that was it.

McKenzie shook her head. "Pays to be rich."

"Sure does."

"Hey, hey! You ladies didn't start without us, did you?" Chase Fredericks asked from outside.

"Hope not. That would be terribly rude," Miles Holbrook commented.

Katherine stepped outside. Two more rental cars had arrived. Standing next to one was Chase, a short, handsome man, wearing a jacket and shirt with no tie. He was her LA-based friend who'd bought Vernon's firearms collection weeks ago and who'd attempted to pick up the items from the music room. The British gentleman, Miles, was tall with dark hair and a long wool coat.

"Welcome, you guys," Katherine said. "Come and take a look."

Everyone greeted each other and asked about flights and such. Within a minute, phones were out and prices bounced back and forth.

# THE FALL OF BLACKSTONE MANSION

During the heat of negotiations, Jordan, on the phone with his attorneys, reminded Katherine, "You know, if you were my director, you could just handle all this without me."

"Still thinking on it."

"Just saying."

When all was said and done, Jordan had accepted the offer from Miles for one million, seven hundred and fifty thousand for the smoking room items. Miles had proudly observed that, unlike in America, many Europeans weren't at all ashamed of enjoying the regular cigar. Katherine remembered that back during her semester abroad in Paris, that stereotype had rung true.

---

Katherine gazed at her empty store. The space had felt so eerie with all that furniture from the mansion packed in together, as if along with them, the items brought all the house's mystery and murderous intrigue. But now that the space's blank walls stared back at her and its slight echo reflected the town's little noises, the store felt even more disconcerting.

She eagerly locked up. She was not about to hang around waiting for Vernon's ghost, or any other, to show up again. *Funny that. Why haven't any of them contacted me lately? It's like they're hiding or waiting for something.*

With the success of the sale, she went to Blackstone's only diner to treat herself to some hot cocoa and maybe a Greek omelet. The diner wasn't anything fancy, but she took great comfort in its food and ever-present server, her friendly acquaintance, Wendy.

"Happy Monday, hon," Wendy said as Katherine sat at the counter.

"Hey, how's it goin'?" Katherine set her purse on the next seat.

"Oh, you know. The usual. Speaking of which, can I get you that?"

"The usual?"

"Yeah."

"Uh-huh. Except toss in a Greek omelet."

"Oh? Celebrating something?" Wendy referred to the fact that the last time Katherine had ordered such, she'd been celebrating locating her current store space.

"Eh, feel like treating myself."

"I'll put it in."

"Hey, Wendy, can I ask you something?"

"Shoot."

"You like your job?"

Wendy gawked at her as if to say "What the hell do *you* think?"

# THE FALL OF BLACKSTONE MANSION

"Sorry," Katherine said, "what I mean is, if someone offered you a job, would you take it?"

"Guess that depends on what it is."

"Director. Of a trust."

"As in the head of the company?" Wendy looked really confused, as if no one offered those kinds of jobs to anybody.

"Yeah."

"It pay good?"

"Yeah."

"Better than antiques?"

"Um, yeah. Kind of."

"I'd say sign me up." Wendy grinned and went to the kitchen to put in Katherine's order.

*She's right. What am I hesitating for?* She took out her phone and looked up area attorneys to find someone to look over the offer letter.

Seconds later, Wendy dropped off her usual mug of hot cocoa. The older woman smiled before attending to other customers.

"Thanks," Katherine said, even though Wendy had already walked away.

Katherine had so far found at least ten listings for attorneys. She narrowed those down to nearby. Zero. *Great. Am I gonna have to drive out to Portland again?* She next narrowed the list by five-star ratings. Now it was five items. She picked the first one.

```
Strandberg, Gold, and Roark
```

She tapped on their site and navigated to a contact form. She made an appointment for the next day afternoon so she wouldn't have to get up too early to drive out.

She soon got e-mail confirmation and a generic message of how happy they were to assist her. She marked the appointment and address on her calendar.

Wendy dropped off the omelet. Katherine ate, thinking about what she might ask these attorneys. *Do I get an expense account so I don't have to submit receipts anymore?*

Finishing her meal, she wasn't sure what to do with the rest of her day. Kirk wouldn't get home for several more hours and she didn't want to take yet another walk around Blackstone's town square. She decided to go back to his apartment and, if nothing else, watch a documentary or two.

Outside, she halted a few feet in front of the diner. A little over a week ago was the first time she'd seen the man in black watching her from the side of one building next to the town square. She looked around, but saw no one suspicious. Only the usual trickle of townsfolk going about their business. *You watched me. You sent me those creepy roses and that awful poem. Was it a power move? Make sure I know you're in control? But to what end? Who are you and what are you doing?*

## THE FALL OF BLACKSTONE MANSION

She gave the town square one last 360, but still saw no men in black. Feeling increasingly exposed the longer she stood out here, she marched to her car and took off.

# 7

"Good afternoon, Ms. Norrington." A tall man with graying temples and a cheap suit offered his hand.

"'Morning." Katherine stood and shook hands.

She was in the law offices of Strandberg, Gold, and Roark, a modest outfit in a giant skyscraper in downtown Portland.

"I'm Michael Roark, partner here. You can call me Michael or, as my kids insist, Mike."

"And I'm Kat."

"Won't you come back?" He led her down the small hallway to his office.

She found a space no bigger than Drew Barrister's at Blackstone Insurance. He was the insurer covering her store and her former landlord before he'd kicked her out after having left a pile of antique firearms in his late father's house. The situation had been a challenge, but after having pretty much bribed him with a donation in his father's name to a conservation charity, he'd been nothing but smiles

# THE FALL OF BLACKSTONE MANSION

and good cheer. Or so she assumed, as she hadn't seen him since.

Michael gestured to the chair opposite his desk. "Please, have a seat." He closed the door.

"Thanks." She sat and took a second to size up his office. Other than a handful of mementos on his desk and graduation certificates on his wall, it was nothing fancy. She doubted her choice of firm. While she wasn't an elitist with most things, she'd found over the years that presentation often did matter in the quality of attorneys. *Eh, all I need him for is document review. Not defense in a murder case.*

"So, as I recall from your message, you needed us to review a contract or...?"

She took Jordan's folded up offer letter out of her purse. While the purse was open, her eyes lingered on the pendant. They must have stayed glued to the piece a little long, as he interrupted with a hint of concern.

"Kat?"

She looked up and handed over the letter. "An offer letter."

He glanced at the text. "Sort of a mix between offer letter and contract."

"What does it sign me up for?"

He lowered the letter. "I should let you know that with this initial, free consultation, I can give you some generalities, but won't be able to go into specifics without a retainer."

*Wonderful. Two hundred and fifty bucks for him to read a couple pages.* "I'm fine with that."

"Okay. It's three hundred dollars an hour. My secretary will print up the paperwork and bill you at the end."

*Three hundred? Have you seen your offices, dude?* "Sounds good."

"All right." He sounded like he was strapping in to the world's most exciting thrill ride. "This is all straight-forward language. You can't spend all his money. You can't badmouth him to the public, on social media."

"How about to friends?"

He stared at her, seeming to wonder if she was serious.

"Kidding," she said.

"Ah." He smiled. "I'm sure a little comment here and there wouldn't be lawsuit-worthy." He read some more. "Good salary."

"Standard?"

"Well, that depends on the company. Steve Jobs famously only took a dollar in salary his second tenure at Apple."

"So the gist?"

"You have full authority to do as you see fit with his trust."

# THE FALL OF BLACKSTONE MANSION

"Really?"

"You can't burn down his mansion, but yes, looks like you have full autonomy."

"No need for approval from the board?"

"No mention of a board."

"He had this big party at the mansion for Halloween. I didn't think it was a great idea. Had this contract been in place at the time, could I have canceled it?"

"Legally speaking, yes, but that would've placed you in direct opposition with your employer."

"So he could've retaliated."

"Could've fired you."

*Maybe I'll cancel Thanksgiving dinner and quit!* "The mansion needs to be completely rewired for electricity. Could I manage that?"

"Absolutely."

*That's why he wants me to be his director. So it's my responsibility to take care of logistics he doesn't wanna deal with.* "Could I order something moved out of the mansion?"

"You mean like furniture?"

"Something more personal." *I can finally bury Vernon and Reginald in the family cemetery. Maybe that'll make sure they stay away.*

"According to this, yes. Again, depending on how personal, Mr. Blackstone may have an issue with it, but legally speaking, yes."

*Wait a minute...* "Could I order a survey of the house?"

"Not sure I understand."

"I dunno what to call it. Hire somebody to make a map of the place."

"Like a floor plan?"

"Yeah. But really specific."

"You could do that for free. Call the county records office."

"Already tried. They had no record."

"Huh." He seemed surprised by that. "According to the text, yes."

*Okay, order wiring and get somebody to tell me what's at the center of those connectors.*

She asked him a few more minor questions about meaningless things like when she could visit the property. She already knew the answers, but figured she might as well fill some more of that three-hundred-dollar hour she was paying for. "Well, Michael, thank you so much for your time." She stood to go.

"Absolutely, Kat. Please, let me walk you out." He stood and opened the door for her.

At reception, he told his secretary to print up a retainer agreement, then turned his full attention to Katherine. "Please don't hesitate to call me day or night with anything, no matter how small."

Katherine signed the agreement. *So you can run up an epic ton of billable hours?* "I will do that, Michael."

"Mike." He smiled wide.
"Thought only your kids called you that."
He chuckled. "Have a great day, Kat."

---

"I'm gonna take the gig," Katherine told Kirk over the phone as she drove back to Creek.

"Even though you didn't want it?"

*He's right. I did make a big fuss over that.* "It's presented certain benefits that I think I wanna take advantage of."

"Like the salary."

"That's one."

"We should celebrate."

"Celebrate my now guaranteed constant interactions with Silver-Spoon Baby?"

"Eh, little adventures."

*That's what I called you and me leaving Oregon for greener pastures. This mean I'm staying here?* "Yeah. Little adventures."

"I'll make reservations."

"Where?"

"It's a surprise."

"Okay. See you tonight."

"Bye." He hung up.

She rang Jordan. He answered immediately.

"Kat! A fine Tuesday morning to you!"

"I'm in."

"In?"

"Just met with an attorney. I will send over the signed offer letter as soon as I get back to town."

"Great! That's wonderful! Glad to have you aboard!"

"Yep."

"Let's celebrate!"

"Um... I kinda just made plans with—"

"Cancel 'em! You, me, your boyfriend, Dirk—"

"Kirk."

"Him too! Fae. C..."

*C? What's she doing there?*

"Portland City Grill tonight at 7:00!"

*Damn it! I wanted to celebrate with Kirk! I guess this is what being a new trust director looks like.* "Okay..." She wanted to come up with an excuse why she couldn't do tonight, but had nothing.

"I'll get us a private room and table service!"

"Do they do that sort of thing? It's not a club."

"They will for me."

She hated how right he was. How he could just roll into any restaurant and order literally whatever he wanted. At the same time, she'd be lying if she said she didn't also enjoy the benefits of being the right hand to the king. "Awesome. I look forward to it." Not quite a lie. She looked forward to a nice meal.

"See you tonight. Seven sharp." He hung up.

# THE FALL OF BLACKSTONE MANSION

She rang Kirk.

"Hey, somethin' go down?" he asked.

She sighed. "I'm really sorry. There's been a change of plans."

## 8

"Good evening, Ms. Norrington," said their impeccably dressed Portland City Grill host. "Your party is waiting for you right over here."

"Ms. Norrington? Again?" Kirk whispered to Katherine.

"Shut up," she whispered back.

The host escorted them past the main dining area, with its panoramic views of the city. He led them up some stairs to the private chef's table, which overlooked the kitchen and had an even better city view.

There they found Jordan, Fae, and Stacey already into a glass of wine and chatting. Jordan wore a nice jacket and white button-down with no tie. Fae wore a very sexy black dress. Stacey was more plainly dressed in another turtleneck, this one charcoal, and jeans.

The moment Jordan lay eyes on Katherine, he shot straight up. "Kat!"

# THE FALL OF BLACKSTONE MANSION

She could tell he was already tipsy. *Maybe more than one glass.* "'Evening, Jordan. Everyone."

Stacey nodded while holding up her wineglass. Fae offered such a small nod, Katherine wasn't sure she even saw her head move.

Jordan stumbled over to meet Katherine and Kirk. "And Picard!"

Kirk grinned. "Other captain."

Jordan repeatedly snapped his fingers. "Right! Uh... Uh... Kirk!"

"There you go."

"Come on! Sit down! Have a glass of wine. Or two," Jordan insisted as he made his way back to his seat.

Katherine and Kirk sat opposite the others.

"Didn't realize it was such a formal evening." Katherine nodded at Fae.

Fae lifted her wineglass and smirked. The nicest reaction she would ever grant Katherine.

"Formal? No, no, no, no, no." Jordan poured himself another glass. "You're the director! You can dress however you damn well please!"

Katherine thought she caught Fae bristling at the word "director," but wondered if she was imagining things. *Not my choice, lady.*

Jordan raised his glass. "To new horizons!"

Stacey and Fae raised their glasses. Kirk poured water for himself and Katherine, and they also joined in.

"New horizons," Katherine said.

They all *clinked*, except Fae, who merely made the gesture of moving her glass closer to the others.

"Tonight's chef's menu, so hope you like... fish." Jordan giggled, maybe at the lack of otherwise presumed choice, given the place was so fancy.

"How you guys doing?" Stacey asked Katherine and Kirk.

*Huh. Surprised she cares. Or at least pretends to. More than Fae seems to be capable of.* "Good." Katherine looked at Kirk for confirmation.

"Yeah. Looking forward to a nice meal."

"Nice?" Jordan asked. "Oh no, my man. PCG makes some of the finest seafood you'll ever have."

*Guessing he's had all that the city, or even region, has to offer, so maybe he's right.*

Stacey squinted at Kirk. "What was it you do again? Antiques too?"

Kirk began, "Oh no. I'm in—"

"Rodekill. The band. He's their drummer." Katherine smiled proudly.

"New band?" Stacey asked.

"No, uh, we've been around a while," Kirk said.

Stacey shook her head. "Huh. Never heard of you."

"We're, uh, up and coming."

"They're a bit of classic Delta blues with a touch of Chicago," Fae offered. "A smidge of mid nineties post-grunge pop-rock."

"That's, uh, pretty accurate, yeah," Kirk agreed.

"Lead's a little uninspired. Mainly Berry-derived licks."

"I'll be sure and tell them."

"Kirk's gonna be on *my* label!" Jordan declared.

"Really?" Stacey sounded genuinely impressed.

Fae touched Stacey's wrist and shook her head.

"Oh..." Stacey nodded.

*Did you have to do that in front of him, Fae?*

Their dedicated server brought up appetizers of grilled Cajun shrimp, then narrated the many details of their preparation. It was fascinating stuff. So much so that Katherine, for a second, wished she'd gone into the culinary arts.

Once the server left, Jordan poured himself his next glass and leaned into the table. "So, Kat, let's talk turkey." He chuckled, then laughed. "Sorry. Just... talk turkey, Thanksgiving." He laughed some more.

"They got it," Fae assured.

"You said foodie influencers, harpists, any other ideas for the day?"

"Actually, I think influencers was your idea," Katherine corrected. She looked at Kirk. *Didn't realize I had to have a full presentation prepared.* "Well, first things first, gotta get the place wired."

"Wired?" Jordan sounded like he'd never heard the word before.

"For electricity?"

Jordan stiffened. For a second, he sounded sober. "Don't worry about that."

*Is he dealing with it?* "You're taking care of it?"

Jordan didn't answer. He was staring past her and Kirk. Off in a different world.

"Will it be ready in time?" Fae had both eyebrows cocked.

"Hope so, since we have, what, two weeks?" Katherine asked.

Kirk nodded.

Jordan's attention returned to the group. He shook his head. "Yeah. It's sure gonna cost me."

"Probably, but don't want the harpists plucking in the dark," Katherine said.

"What about catering?"

Katherine stared at him. *I have no earthly idea, Jordan! The meals we don't make or order in I have at the diner!* "Um, I can certainly look into the five-star places in the area." She knew that sounded woefully pathetic, but didn't know what else to say at the moment. *You did accept the position.*

Fae offered, "Babe, I know all the top chefs. I can call—"

Jordan's tone was dismissive, almost to the point of being mean. "I asked my director."

Fae bit her lip, then downed a half glass of wine.

# THE FALL OF BLACKSTONE MANSION

Katherine attempted to throw Fae a bone. "You know, I would love Fae's input. She knows so much more about this than I do."

Fae lowered her head a full inch so she could give Katherine a good, hard eye roll. Her expression seemed to say "Thanks, bitch, I'm good." She'd displayed a similar one both to Katherine and Kirk at the Halloween party. Katherine had a hunch this wouldn't be the last time.

"I love Thanksgiving! All the food!" Stacey contributed.

Fae threw her a look, but that was it. Jordan said nothing.

*Poor girl. Way over her head. What is she doing here, anyway? I get Jordan wanting to connect with family, but...*

"I know you'll figure it out," Jordan told Katherine. "You always do."

After they'd just finished their first course, Katherine scooted her chair from the table. "Think I'd better hit the little girl's room."

"Same here," Fae said.

"Me too!" Stacey said.

*Great. I have to go, but now they're gonna... I don't even know what.*

"So, Kirk, you sure know how to whack them sticks," Jordan started as the ladies headed down the stairs.

Katherine threw Kirk a worried look, but he smiled.

Entering the bathroom, she retreated into a stall before either Fae or Stacey would have time to say anything. After finishing, she hung out for another half minute. She heard another toilet flush and footsteps leave. Hoping that was Fae, she exited her stall.

Fae was right there waiting for her. Blocking the sinks.

"Excuse me." Katherine stepped around her.

"Director," Fae said.

"Yep." Katherine scrubbed her hands quickly.

"You know, he never asked me. Never even suggested it. Even though I've been running my own successful company for over ten years now."

"Maybe that's something you should bring up with him." Katherine wiped her hands. As she turned to leave, she felt a firm grip on her arm.

Fae glared at her. "What's your angle?"

"I dunno what you're talking about."

"You wanna screw him?"

"No."

"You're not missing much. I mean, he has his moments, but definitely not the best lay I've ever had."

"I really don't need to know."

"Hoping to become the next Mrs. Blackstone?"

## THE FALL OF BLACKSTONE MANSION

"Fae, I only want..." *Access to the mansion so I can figure out what's up with those tombs and why Marcus murdered his family, and... and all that other stuff!*

"What?"

"I don't want anything from him. All I ever wanted was to sell his antiques, make a decent commission, and..."

"So why'd you accept the position?"

*Because... Wait. Why the hell should I tell you?* "We better get back." She attempted to remove her arm from Fae's grasp.

Fae didn't lift her fingers. "We're not done."

"Okay..."

Fae marched out.

When Katherine returned to the table, everyone, even Fae, was all smiles and laughter. Katherine must have been wearing a sour expression because the second she sat, Kirk leaned into her.

"Everything okay?" he asked quietly.

"Yeah. Tell ya later."

---

After dinner, which Katherine had to admit had been amazing, Jordan led everyone outside. "So, where to next?"

The others chuckled politely. Katherine took the moment of group distraction to scan for the man in black. She saw no one.

"Some of us have our own businesses to run." Fae's eyes stabbed daggers at Katherine.

"And then there's the working class," Stacey said.

"Second that," Kirk said.

"Kat! You and me!" Jordan threw his arms wide open.

"I'm with the working class." Katherine wrapped her arm around Kirk.

"Well, I'm not gonna go drinking alone," Jordan moped.

"Looks like you're stuck with the plebes." Fae hooked her arm around his elbow.

Jordan didn't even look at her. He did, though, look at Stacey. "Need a ride?"

"I was just gonna grab a bus." Stacey eyed Fae.

"Forget that, C! We'll drop you off," Jordan declared.

"Um, all right."

"We're this way," Jordan informed Katherine.

"And we're this way." Katherine pointed in the opposite direction.

"Have a good night," Fae said conclusively.

Jordan and Stacey expressed similar sentiments, and the trio left in their direction.

"He mentioned his label again," Kirk confided in Katherine.

"Really?"

"Yeah. I wonder if he's serious."

"He may intend to be, but I'd still keep my expectations low."

"Made you director."

"Yeah, well, I still don't quite understand that."

"Low expectations."

She squeezed him. "Let's get outta here."

"After you."

## 9

Katherine shot straight up in bed.

"Not quite yet," Kirk mumbled.

He was right. According to her phone, it was only 7:45. He still had fifteen minutes before he needed to get up. She, being the Blackstone trust's new director, could get up whenever, so long as she got things done.

Yet she was so accustomed to Jordan's early morning calls buzzing her out of deep sleeps, she'd kept coming to several minutes early in anticipation.

She lay back down.

"That's it." Kirk wrapped his arm around her.

She groaned. "I just know he's gonna..."

"Probably, but right now, you've got at least another thirteen minutes of peace," Kirk assured her.

"Yeah." She rubbed her cheek into his shoulder.

Those remaining thirteen minutes of peace raced by at terrifying speed. The very next thing she knew, he was getting ready for work.

She picked up her phone, expecting that at any second, Jordan would call.

He didn't.

"Have a good one." Kirk leaned in to kiss her goodbye.

"You too." She kissed him.

As she heard the door close, she swung her legs out of bed and threw on her clothes. *First full day. I wonder...* She tapped her bank's app on her phone. She was very surprised to see that Jordan had been true to his word. Her first monthly payment had already gone through. "Crap. Guess I gotta earn it."

She opened her laptop on the dining table, and looked up Portland General Electric's contact information. Locating a number, she gave it a ring.

A pleasant young male voice answered. "Business accounts. This is Jeff."

"Hey, Jeff, my name's Kat. I'm calling because I need to check on the process of hooking up a property I'm sort of in charge of."

"Address?"

"Probably one Promontory in Blackstone—something like that—eastern Clackamas county."

She heard him tap on his keyboard. "Yeah. I gotcha," he said. "Looks like this job is well underway."

"Really?"

"Enterprise team and everything."

"You sound surprised."

"Well, normally, such a large team and tight deadline would be reserved for government contracts, like if, I dunno, a new DMV or post office were being built in the middle of nowhere and they needed to quickly connect it to the grid."

"I see. What's the deadline? The twenty-fourth?"

"Actually, a little earlier. The eighteenth."

"Does it say why that date?"

"Nope. Just that it's a firm deadline. Client insisted the work be done by then."

*I guess Jordan wanted plenty of wiggle room to have the place ready by Thanksgiving.* "Jeff, can you add my number to the file? I'm the director of the trust that's funding the job, so should probably be in the loop."

"Yep. Whenever you're ready."

She gave him her number, and they wrapped up the conversation. *The eighteenth, huh? And if they don't finish by then?* One aspect of being Jordan's director that was only now dawning on her was the notion that he could and likely would blame literally anything on her that didn't work out to his immediate satisfaction. While she was used to his little tantrums that were outside of her control, getting used to any that would result from things inside her control would take some adjustment.

# THE FALL OF BLACKSTONE MANSION

*Enterprise team?* Two birds. She needed to head out anyway to check on the wiring installation. She might as well also get a floor plan drawn up. "Find out what else is buried there." Since she wasn't sure what was required for that, she had to try a few internet searches before she landed on a freelancer site and a handful of draftspersons.

She picked the first one with a five-star rating and sent an e-mail.

```
Hi Maya,
Looking for someone to draw up a floor
 plan of existing, very large rural proper-
 ty. That in your wheelhouse? Lemme know.
 Kat.
```

With the message sent, her eyes shot straight to her purse. *I don't have to go right now. Should wait a bit to see if I hear back from Maya.* She sat on the couch right next to her purse and stared down at it. She placed her hand on it, about to open it, when her eyes lifted to the door. *Kirk won't be back for hours,* she thought, at the possibility of him catching her.

She feverishly unzipped her purse and yanked out the pendant. She heard a relieved sigh escape her lips as she lifted it up. "Yeah." She clutched the piece in her left hand and ran her right index finger from the V's tip up to the triangle's top point. The action was extremely satisfying, like the first slug of a cold beer after a hot day out in the sun. She ran her finger back down to the V's point. She did this a few more times before she realized how strange it would have looked to anyone who suddenly walked in on her. Anyone like Kirk.

Feeling self-conscious, she set the pendant on top of her purse, but kept stroking it. "Maybe I should... Maybe..." She had the powerful desire to know more about it, its origins and intended purpose, but the more she thought about it, the more her thoughts swirled into an incoherent soup. The only point of focus she could achieve was how much she wanted to spend the rest of the day touching its mysterious black metal.

*Buzz!* Her phone vibrated in her pocket. She felt a jolt of shame, as if the caller on the other end could somehow see her caressing the pendant.

She took out her phone and checked the ID, expecting it to be Jordan, with the latest round of irritations all ready for her.

It was an e-mail message from the draftswoman, Maya.

```
So in my wheelhouse! Can totally draw up
a floor plan for you. Address? Availabil-
ity? Please feel free to reach out any
time.
```

She left her number and e-mail address.

# THE FALL OF BLACKSTONE MANSION

Katherine put the pendant back in her purse, zipped it up, and called Maya's number.

"Hello?" a curious female voice answered.

"Hey, Maya. It's Kat."

"Oh, hey, that was quick."

"Figured might as well jump on this."

"You need a floor plan."

"That's right."

"For your house?" Maya's tone sounded like she wanted the answer to be no.

"No."

"I was gonna say, could just call the county or builders."

"Yeah, no, this is the house of my employer. Mansion, actually. I run his trust."

"Trust?"

"Yep."

"As in, like, oil barons and banking empires?"

"That's right."

"Must be a big place."

"It's sizable. So what's your availability?"

"What's your deadline?"

"As soon as possible."

"Oh, well, in that case..."

"What's your rate?"

Maya sounded like she was pulling the number out of thin air. "Three hundred an hour."

"Start today and I'll double it." Katherine figured if there was any benefit to running a trust, it was getting stuff done.

"Sure. Where's the site?"

Katherine gave her the pertinent information.

"Wow, that's way out there!" Maya said.

"How soon can you meet me?"

"I'm in Wilsonville, so it'll be about an hour and twenty."

"See you then."

## 10

On her way to the mansion, Katherine kept checking her mirrors for any sign of the man in black. She figured if he was going to hang out in alleys across from where she was trying to enjoy an evening with her boyfriend, he probably wouldn't pause to follow her around as she went about her day.

Yet she saw no sign of anything suspicious. No cars trailing her. No hats peeking around corners.

She recognized the ever-present twilight as she drove along the road through the forest only seconds away from the mansion. She hadn't seen the phenomenon since two weeks earlier when she was last here during the daytime. *Wonder if I'll ever know why it looks like that up here?*

Rounding the last bend before the last stretch of road to the house's gate, she slammed on the brakes. "What the hell is all this?" she asked the view through her windshield.

## AUGUSTINE PIERCE

A caravan of PGE vans and trucks had parked all along the road up to the six-foot high, black-brick wall that surrounded the property. It was nearly the number of vehicles as there had been for the Halloween party. An army of electricians, general contractors, and other workers swarmed the hill.

Lacking a nearer option, she parked in a length of unobstructed road right in front of a truck. Stepping out of her car, she braced at the cold, ten degrees lower than in town. After a good minute-long walk, she passed a small silver sedan and Jordan's obnoxious blue Ferrari. *What's he doing here?* At the gate, she stepped aside as a few workers passed by, carrying wooden poles, wire coils, construction tools, and various other supplies.

Passing through, she did her best to stay out of the way. She peered up at the mansion, at its monstrous four stories of solid black stone and three visible conical towers looming over the hill. She turned her attention to the west, toward the town. The PGE team had already erected a power line leading from the back of the house, and worming deep into the woods. It looked exactly like the kind built along the side of any ordinary suburban street. *PGE guy wasn't kidding. This is a massive job.*

"Not much to look at, especially next to J's ride, but she gets me from A to B," Stacey said.

# THE FALL OF BLACKSTONE MANSION

Katherine jumped and spun around. Stacey stood just beyond the gate, looking profoundly bored.

"Hey. 'Morning," Katherine greeted.

"'Morning."

"She?"

Stacey pointed past the gate to the sedan. "My girl."

"Oh, uh, A to B. Good." Katherine wove through the stream of workers to join her. "Sorry, C, none of my business, but don't you have work?"

"I'm at work."

"Jordan's buying flowers for the mansion?"

Stacey laughed. "Oh, I ditched that gig like a clingy boyfriend."

"You did?" Katherine was surprised at her cheerful attitude toward being unemployed.

"Yeah. This pays a *lot* better."

"What's this?"

"I'm assisting J now."

"Oh, didn't realize he needed an assistant."

"Yeah. It's actually really easy. Just, ya know, get him stuff, make calls for him, that sorta thing. J says he's grooming me to be his right-hand man—uh, woman. Honestly, not too different from what I did at the flower shop. Only pays a *lot* more."

*Yeah, you mentioned that.* "Awfully generous of a fifth cousin."

"Actually, fifth—Oh. Sorry. So used to correcting him. Yeah, I mean, neither of us has any immediate family or, ya know, partner, so... Well, I guess he has Fae, but, I mean, come on."

"Yeah. So where is he?"

Stacey pointed up the hill. "With the electric guys. Back of the house."

"Why are you down here?"

Stacey shrugged. "Nothin' for me to do up there."

*Fair enough, C.* "Think I could peek at the progress?"

"Fine by me," Stacey said cheerfully.

*With a gatekeeper like you...* "Cool. Probably see you again in a sec once I get bored too."

"I'll be here."

Katherine hiked up the coal-black cobblestone road up to the carriage circle in front of the mansion's entrance, then around to the back. There she found dozens of workers, a brand-new fuse box, a column of scaffolding up the building's side, and Jordan exchanging some intense words with three bearded men in PGE coveralls.

The fuse box particularly grabbed her attention. The last time she was up here, then with Jordan and an electrician, when they'd opened the previous box, itself over a century old, they'd found that someone had completely destroyed all its innards. Most likely with an ax.

# THE FALL OF BLACKSTONE MANSION

"You said it'd be done by the eighteenth!" Jordan barked at the men.

"That was an estimate, Mr. Blackstone," the man on the left said.

*Hm. Maybe I should hang back for a sec.* She gazed up at the scaffolding. The workers had set it up to support the installation of a thick wire that stretched from the top of the fuse box straight up the side of the wall, all the way to the roof. *Weird configuration.* She threw a glance over at the power line. From what she could tell, electricity would flow directly from the grid to the roof. *For satellite TV? Maybe he wants it for the Thanksgiving influencers.*

Jordan sighed. "That is *not* what you guys told me over the phone. I was told it would be *done*."

"With all due respect, Mr. Blackstone, we can never be completely certain," the man on the right said. "There are always variables. The woods, for one, are much thicker than expected."

"So cut 'em down!" Jordan bellowed.

*Maybe I should make myself scarce. I don't think anyone's noticed me yet.*

"We can only do that to the edge of your property," the middle man said. "After that, it requires permission from the owner. Or, in the case of the county, a permit."

"So get a permit!" Jordan insisted.

*Yeah, I'm definitely gonna make myself scarce.* She turned around and started her way back to Stacey.

"Well, Mr. Blackstone, that'd be up to you and your office," Mr. Left said.

*Actually, probably up to me. What fun.*

"Fine!" Jordan yelled. "Fine. Whatever. Fine. Kat? What are *you* doing here?"

Katherine froze and turned around. Jordan looked so perplexed, it was as if she'd appeared out of thin air.

"Uh, checking up on things?" she asked.

Jordan took a few steps toward her. "Thought I told you not to worry about the electricity."

"Not worried at all. Just figured, as your director, I should be aware of the progress."

He glared at her for a second, as if he knew she'd stolen something from him, but couldn't prove it. He then gazed up at the scaffolding. "It's progressing."

*What's with the wire?* "Great to hear. Guess I'll see how C's doing." She did *not* want to clue him into the draftswoman, who'd soon arrive.

He didn't return his attention to her yet. "Stacey's fine. If, as my director, you're looking for something to do, why don't you lock down a caterer?" He finally faced her.

"I thought Fae knew all the top chefs in the Portland area."

# THE FALL OF BLACKSTONE MANSION

"Fae's not my director. You are." He turned his attention back to the scaffolding.

"Well, then, I guess I'll start searching. Maybe show a prospective around. Any particular preference?"

"For what?"

"Caterers."

"You know what I like."

*No I don't, Jordan! That's why I'm asking!* "I'll find some options."

"I'm sure you will." He faced her. "Keep me updated." By which, he clearly meant "Get lost."

"One other little thing?"

He sighed with complete exasperation. "Yes?"

"I know it's none of my business—"

"Spit it out, Kat."

"What's with C?"

"What do you mean?"

"You find her outta the blue, wine and dine her, then hire her as your assistant?"

The corners of his lips lifted into a smirk. "You two've been gossiping!"

"It's like she's your new best friend."

"Well, ya know, Kat. No siblings. No parents. No close cousins. Found C. Figured family's family, right?"

"I guess."

"Anything else?"

She shook her head. "Guess I'll see about those caterers."

"You do that." Turning his back to her, he rejoined the electricians.

She headed down the hill. Reaching Stacey, she took out her phone to check the time. It was still about another half hour before Maya arrived.

"Find Jordan?" Stacey asked.

"Yeah," Katherine replied.

"Something wrong?"

"Sorry?"

"You seem troubled."

"You know what they're doing up there?"

"Hooking up electricity."

*Yeah, C, I know that part.* "I mean, does anything seem strange about how they're going about it?"

Stacey shrugged. "I dunno anything about electrical engineering."

"I don't know much about it either. Looks like they're installing something on the roof."

"Weather vein?"

"Maybe. He ever mention why the eighteenth is so important?"

Stacey shook her head. "Just that it's the deadline."

"Right. Well, I gotta go wait for someone."

Stacey perked up. "Who's that?"

# THE FALL OF BLACKSTONE MANSION

*Crap. If I tell her, she'll probably tell Jordan, and he'll ask all kinds of questions.* "Um, just a friend I'm showin' around."

"Wow, cool! Can I come?"

*No, then you'd* definitely *tell him what I'm up to!* "What if Jordan came looking for you? Wouldn't wanna get you in trouble."

Stacey nodded slowly, likely thoroughly considering those implications. "Right. Good point. Thanks for lookin' out."

Katherine gave her a thumbs up. "We Blackstone employees gotta stick together."

"Exactly!"

Before Stacey could think of any other questions, observations, or self-invitations, Katherine exited to the PGE caravan and walked its length to wait for Maya.

After twenty minutes, a butterscotch-colored VW bug arrived. A petite brunette stepped out. She had a backpack slung over one shoulder.

Katherine waved.

"Wow! We are *out* here!" Maya said.

"Sure are." Katherine met her half way and shook her hand.

"Is it me or is it dark enough to almost be nighttime up here?"

"It's not you."

"The woods blocking out the daylight?"

Katherine shook her head. *No idea.*
"And it is *cold*!" Maya rubbed her arms.
Katherine nodded. "About ten lower than in town."
They'd almost reached the gate when Maya paused to take in its enormity. "Sizable?"
"And that's just the gate." Katherine motioned for her to pass through.
The second Maya entered, Stacey waved and greeted her. "Hey!"
Maya waved back timidly. "Hey."
Katherine rushed through the introductions as she directed Maya up the hill. "Stacey, Maya. Maya, Stacey."
Stacey began, "Call me C—"
Katherine interrupted. "Stacey's Jordan's assistant and Maya's eager to get to it."
"Nice to meet you," Stacey called after them.
"You too." Maya smiled, then asked Katherine. "Who's Jordan?"
"Owner of the trust."
"Of which you're the head?"
"That's right." *I guess.*
"What's that entail?"
"So far, phone calls."
Maya chuckled. "To draftswomen."
"Exactly."
"Are you guys gonna build an addition?"

# THE FALL OF BLACKSTONE MANSION

"Not as far as I know."

"Usually the only reason to have a plan drawn up is because the owner intends to make significant alterations, like an addition."

"The building is old enough that the county doesn't have records. We're planning events and I figured it'd be better to have as much information as possible, to, ya know, help catering orient themselves in the space." *Talk about out of thin air. Eh, seems plausible enough.*

"Oh my God!" Maya exclaimed as the mansion came into full view.

"Yep."

"That thing's... enormous!"

"Wait till you see the inside."

Maya halted. "Look, it was really generous of you to offer double my rate, but you should know, this is gonna take a while."

"Like, how long?"

"Honestly, I don't know, but a three-bedroom house takes an average of ten hours, so yeah."

"Don't worry about it."

"You sure?"

Katherine nodded emphatically. "Let's get to it."

They soon reached the front doors.

Maya halted again, lifting her eyes all the way to the top of the entryway hall's tower. "Wow."

"How does this work?"

Maya hadn't yet lowered her eyes. "Start from the outside. Work our way in."

*Great. Won't know what's in the center till the end.* "Is it necessary to get *every* square inch of the outside?"

Maya gawked at her. "How accurate do you wanna be?"

*Fair question, especially since I mentioned caterers.* "Of course. I just thought with the other work going on..."

"I noticed. Where's that happening?"

"Mostly the back, but I really don't wanna get in their way."

"I guess we can do the front and then head in."

"Great. Where do we start?"

Maya pointed at the line between the two front doors. She took out an iPad and a palm-sized black device. "Laser measuring tool."

"Looks very sci-fi."

Maya grinned. "Oh, it is."

"After the front doors, that way?" Katherine pointed to the right. Much like with the electrician from weeks ago, she didn't want Maya's attention to fall on the family cemetery, and thus possibly inundate her with questions. If Maya were already facing the house taking measurements, that'd minimize the likelihood that she'd discover the burial ground.

"Good as any."

"Better lighting."

# THE FALL OF BLACKSTONE MANSION

Maya set up her first measurement, placing her tool against where the left door's left edge met the stone wall. "This is gonna be awhile." She locked eyes with Katherine. "Like, a long while. So don't feel obligated to stick around."

"Yeah. Of course. Um..." Katherine scanned the woods as if a picnic table would magically present itself. *I can't just leave her here. What if Jordan finds her, or worse, one of the Blackstones descends upon her? But I can't hover either.* She offered Maya a smile. "I'll be around."

She started down the hill. Remembering a crucial detail, she called back to Maya. "Hey, sorry to interrupt, but forgot to tell you, cell coverage is crap up here, so if you need anything, just holler."

"Sounds good! Thanks!"

Remembering Stacey at the gate, Katherine parked in the middle of the carriage loop. She took out her phone, sat on the ground, and fired up *Fruit Ninja*.

---

After countless rounds of slicing fruit to bits on her mobile while seated in the middle of the mansion's carriage circle, Katherine heard Maya's approaching voice.

"This is one weird house," Maya said.

Katherine scrambled to her feet. "Yeah?" She didn't want to reveal what she already knew about the mansion and possibly bias Maya against what she'd learned.

Maya put away her iPad and measuring tool. "It's got these towers that look almost Norman in design, with their conical roofs." She held her arms above her head at a point. "But then it's got all these Greek capitals. It's like…"

"Yeah?" Katherine was so desperate to learn anything new about the mansion that she practically wanted to shake it out of her.

"It's like the Winchester house."

"Really?"

"Ever been there?"

Katherine shook her head. "No."

"Old lady Winchester—forget her name—she became obsessed with this idea that once the house was finished being built, she'd die, so she kept adding stuff to it. Stairways, hallways, entire wings. She had all that Winchester money, so she could just keep going."

"Did it work?" Katherine grinned.

"Nah, but she made it to the ripe old age of eighty-six."

"Not a bad run. So Blackstone reminded you of Winchester?"

## THE FALL OF BLACKSTONE MANSION

"Not the same situation, but okay, the towers and capitals? Totally incongruous. Don't match architecturally. Almost like the builder threw it all together."

"That was probably Silas Blackstone. And yeah, from the very little I know about the guy, he was definitely eccentric."

"It wasn't only the incongruous elements."

"Oh?"

Maya took out her iPad and showed Katherine the early stage of a plan. A thick black line drew the outline of the mansion's façade in the style of a pencil sketch on grid paper. With a thinner line, she'd drawn out a guess at the rest. There was a rectangle, the west and east towers, and the familiar V-shape, ending in the entryway hall on the bottom. "I know this sounds crazy, and it's incomplete, but it almost looks like..."

"Yeah?"

"Almost like a symbol."

"Huh." Katherine tried to sound as neutral as possible. She didn't want to let on that she agreed with Maya, but also wanted her to continue.

"You don't see it?" Maya sounded desperate to be believed.

*Oops. That sounded too indifferent.* "Oh yeah, definitely. Wanna check out the inside?"

"Yeah! Absolutely!"

## AUGUSTINE PIERCE

Katherine pulled the front doors wide open. "Let's go."

## 11

The mansion's interior was as dark as the first time Katherine had entered it. *Jordan's taking all that care to wire the house, but couldn't be bothered to start with the friggin' front door?* The house was also far quieter than she would have expected with all the work going on. In fact, it was silent. Not a single thumping hammer or grinding drill. *Really is like a different world in here.*

She took out her flashlight, though was very careful not to open her purse wide enough for Maya to see the pendant. "Sorry. Thought they'd already taken care of the lights."

"No problem."

Katherine clicked on her flashlight.

Maya gasped. "Wow!"

"Yeah."

Maya put away her iPad. "Who *were* these people?"

"Just your average, everyday"—*murderous*—"billionaires."

"Katherine, this is gonna take..." Maya's eyes swam all over the entryway hall. They soon landed on the giant staircase that separated the black marble statues of Artemis and Apollo, posed in knocked-arrow stances aimed at each other. "A while."

"I understand." *Gotta reel her in.* "Considering future events, we're particularly interested in farther inside."

"So we're skipping this?" Maya pointed at the staircase.

"Just wanna, you know, focus."

"Okay. Lead the way."

Katherine led her deeper into the mansion. Maya took a handful of measurements to keep her plan oriented.

Katherine announced their location. "This is the main west-east hallway. At least I think it's the main. Feels like that."

"This where you wanted me to start?"

"Yeah, the kitchen's a few doors down, so we'll mainly be in this area." *Gotta give her a reason to figure out the center of the house.* "But we're interested in being acquainted with as much of the mansion as possible for future events."

"So, then, why don't you want me to measure the entire house from outside in?"

# THE FALL OF BLACKSTONE MANSION

"Because the kitchen and dining room are more immediate." *Now stop questioning the obviously very spotty and selective floor plan!*

Maya nodded. She took measurements of their current intersection. "The kitchen?"

"Right this way." Katherine opened the kitchen door wide. She recalled the first time, weeks ago, when she'd first entered this space. She hadn't known it then, but it was during that time that Eileen's ghost had reached out to her.

"Wow. Very, very nice. Gonna be some outstanding events."

Katherine waited impatiently while Maya took measurements of the kitchen. It seemed like it was taking longer than the whole of the front. Finally, Katherine let her into the dining room.

"Yeah. Wow. I'd love to eat dinner every night in here," Maya said.

*Unless you're about to be murdered.* Katherine thought back to not only Eileen's death, but Gloria's, which had also occurred here. "It's very comfortable."

Maya took her measurements. "So was that it for the rooms you needed immediately?"

"Yeah."

"Where to now?"

"Let's go..." Katherine had no idea where to point her next. *The tombs all connect at the center of the house.*

At least, that's what she assumed. It's what made sense, given what she'd seen. *The center. No, I can't just tell her that. She's already mentioned twice starting on the outside and moving in. She'll think it's weird.* "Um..." She eyed all three of the dining room's entrances, the one to the west-east hallway, the one to the kitchen, and the final one. "Let's go that way." She pointed to the exit that led deeper into the house.

The door opened onto a much narrower west-east hallway than the one she'd seen so many times. She looked left and right, but saw nothing distinct. Each side had a row of doors, most likely leading to more salons, like those of which she'd already seen so many.

Maya got to measuring.

"No. Let's, uh, keep going," Katherine said.

"Shouldn't I at least get some reference so I can connect them later?"

"Don't worry about that now. We can always come back."

Maya nodded.

Katherine didn't know which door was better, so she picked the one in front of her.

As she'd predicted, it was a salon like the others. It had the usual sofas and chairs, with no features that jumped out at her.

"Should I...?" Maya held up her measuring tool as she stepped in.

# THE FALL OF BLACKSTONE MANSION

"Yeah. Go ahead." Katherine scanned the room for anything out of the ordinary.

"Wow. Doesn't quit, does it?"

"You get used to it." Katherine sounded far more frustrated than she'd intended, but she wasn't focusing on how impressive the Blackstones' fortune had been. She wanted answers to all the questions she'd stacked up over the past two months, and she wanted them now.

Yet this salon gave her nothing. Nothing at all. It had no symbols like the towers. It had no sliding bookshelf like the hidden study above Vernon's tomb. *Great. Just gonna have to keep moving forward.*

She stepped toward the other side of the room. *Wait.* She froze and double checked where she was standing. The exit to the hallway was about six feet behind her.

It was the only one.

Katherine double checked the other three walls. There were no other doors. "How deep into the house are we?"

"Can't be sure 'cause my measurements are incomplete—"

"Guess, Maya."

Maya checked her iPad. "A quarter? Maybe a third?"

"We're only a quarter into the floor space of the mansion and we can't go any more."

Maya's voice hesitated while she checked her notes. "Uh... Looks that way."

Katherine stood right up next to the blank wall opposite the entrance and pressed her ear hard against the wallpaper. "What do you hear?"

Maya joined her. "Sounds..."

"Hollow."

Maya nodded. "Yeah."

Deep inside the wall, from many yards away, there arose a low *groan*. It lasted several seconds. In its last moments, it drifted closer.

*That Vernon? What's he want now? Other than to scare off my draftswoman?*

Maya stepped away from the wall. Her brow furrowed with deep concern. "What was that?"

*That look. I had the same one the first time I heard Eileen.* Her mind scrambled for a satisfactory answer. "Probably the machines outside."

"Didn't sound like a machine. Sounded almost—"

"Follow me. Grab whatever measurements you can, but don't worry about it."

"Oh. Okay."

Katherine exited into the narrow hallway and opened the door to the neighboring room. She shone her light across to the opposite wall.

No door.

Katherine repeated the process for the next three rooms. The same result each time. There was no way to access the center of the house. "Those connectors lead *somewhere*."

"Connectors?"

"Nothing. Let's go to the other side."

"Of the house?"

"Yeah." Katherine kept going until they reached an intersection that met another corridor at a hard angle. This new corridor felt very familiar.

"So weird."

"What's that?"

"The angle of these hallways."

"Oh yeah. That. You get used to it."

"I can see why you wanted a floor plan. Impossible to navigate this labyrinth without one."

Katherine didn't respond to her observation, rather she kept going down the current corridor. It would meet a larger hallway, with the same dimensions as the west-east one, that would ultimately lead to the north tower. From there, she'd head directly south toward the front of the house, working her way through rooms until she'd come to another dead end. That would at least give her a rough area of the center that she couldn't reach.

"What is it you're looking for?" Maya asked as they reached the north tower's entrance.

"Looking?"

"Yeah. You're obviously looking for something."

"No, I..." Katherine didn't want to lie to her, but really didn't want to fill her in. What would follow would be a barrage of questions that would most likely lead directly to her storming out. "It's complicated."

Maya looked harshly suspicious. "You do work for the Blackstone trust, right?"

"Absolutely. Sometimes to my great annoyance."

"So this isn't one of those things where you led me out here under the pretense of a floor plan just to murder me?"

"What? Is that what you've been thinking?"

"I haven't known *what* to think, but we are in this giant mansion, in the middle of the creepy woods and you offered me a bunch of money to draw up a plan that you, well, keep telling me not to draw up."

"All you need to know..." Katherine had no idea how to continue. "Look, the Blackstones have a very storied history. Like, *very* storied. Over the last weeks of working with the current heir, Jordan, I've discovered a few things."

"Like what?"

"Doesn't matter."

"Kat, I think I need to know a little, so I don't feel quite so much like you led me out here to murder me."

"Jordan's great-whatever grand-uncle murdered his would-be fiancée."

# THE FALL OF BLACKSTONE MANSION

"Oh my God."

"That's only the beginning."

"Seriously?"

"Yes, and we seriously don't have time for all of it, but in order to get to more of it, I need to know about the mansion's floor plan."

That seemed to calm Maya down. "Okay. So, this isn't really about upcoming events?"

"I mean, kinda, but no, not entirely."

"It's about some old murder."

"Kinda. Yes."

"Well, if I'm helping solve a murder..."

"In a way, you would be. Yes." Katherine was immensely relieved to have found a concrete reason for her to continue, hopefully with no further probing questions. "Now, can you point me to a likely room that'll be about as deep into the house from the north side as the ones we were just in were from the south side?"

Maya stared at her iPad. "Yeah. I think." She pointed in the direction from which they'd come. "Probably third door down. We can start there."

They retreated three doors and Katherine swung it wide open. The room had doors on all four walls.

Maya offered a sheepish smirk. "Maybe the next one?"

"Way ahead of you." Katherine walked to the room's south side, opened that door, and shone her light onto the wall on the other side of the next room.

It was blank.

"Boo-yah." Katherine pressed her ear against the blank wall. *Leave us alone, Vern. We're actually getting somewhere!*

Maya joined her.

They nodded and spoke the word at the same time. "Hollow."

*And I don't hear Vernon coming.* "There is something in there. What could it be?"

"Are you... asking me?"

"Yes!"

"How would I know?"

"You're the architect!"

Maya shook her head. "I'm only a draftswoman!"

"You have studied architecture, though?"

"Yeah, but..."

"Then what do you think?"

"I don't know." Maya looked over her notes on her iPad. "Could be anything. Storage space. Wine cellar."

"Not a goddamn wine cellar. How big's the space?"

"Kat, I didn't take full measurements."

"How big do you *think*? Max?"

"Um... Out of thousands of square feet, looks like it's about a ninth of the total floor space, so at least hundreds."

"Hundreds." Katherine thought back to her time spent in each of the tombs below each of the towers. "Another tomb?"

"Tomb? What are you talking about—?"

"But who could it be for? Marcus was the only other one. Wasn't in the cemetery. Is it his? Why would he build himself a tomb, then abandon the mansion?"

"Kat, you're starting to freak me out."

"All the other ones were underground. Why is this one at ground level?" Katherine lifted her eyes to the ceiling. "Or higher?"

"Kat, seriously?"

A low, deep *groan* echoed in the distance.

*Great. There he is. Couldn't just leave us be.*

"That was *not* a machine."

"We need to go."

The *groan* returned, but this time, it sounded much closer. Only feet away.

*He's following us. Is he really gonna contact me now? In here? With her?*

"Go where?" Maya asked.

A chill swept through the room like an arctic breeze.

"Ow!" Maya nearly dropped her iPad as she rubbed her shoulders.

Then came the stench. That awful, rotten-flesh stench.

"Oh God! What *is* that?" Maya asked.

"Follow me," Katherine instructed. "Keep your eyes on me. Do *not* look back."

"Okay...?" Maya put her iPad and measuring tool in her backpack.

"Let's go." Katherine seized her hand and dragged her out as fast as she could.

"Hey! Careful!" Maya complained.

Katherine ignored her as, directly behind them, she heard that *groan* echo down the hallways every step of the way. That chill nipped at her back. That smell churned her stomach.

A handful of feet remained between them and the open front doors.

Katherine still gripped Maya's hand. "Almost there."

Shooting through, Katherine was relieved to see the woods' twilight. They were outside. Safe. At least as far as she knew. She released Maya's hand.

"What was—?" Maya asked.

The doors slammed shut behind them.

## 12

"What are you doing?" Jordan asked Katherine over the phone. His tone was harshly terse. He also sounded distracted, as if he were also in the middle of a conversation with someone else.

She sat on the couch in Kirk's apartment, her laptop open before her. Her gaze hung on Maya's invoice sitting in her e-mail's inbox. The amount was, surprisingly, the original quote, not double that, which Katherine had offered. She'd thought to question it, but instead submitted the invoice to Jordan's people, believing it to be a straight-forward transaction.

Ten minutes later, he'd called.

"What are you talking about?" Katherine asked him.

"You hired a draftsman?"

"Well, woman, but yes."

"Why?"

Here was where Katherine had minimal confidence in her ability to sell him on her reasoning. "I figured it'd be good to have an official floor plan with the actual measurements of—"

"The caterers can deal with that. I'm canceling this."

"Wait. You're canceling—?"

"Yes, Kat. As in not paying it."

"What about her work?"

"Since you authorized it..."

*Wonderful. On the hook again.*

"How's the catering coming?" he asked.

"I haven't had a chance—"

He sighed, still sounding very distracted.

"Are you with somebody?" she asked.

"No," he answered defensively. "Why would you ask me that?"

"Just sounds like... Whatever. Doesn't matter."

"Update me as soon as you can."

"Will do—" She heard his end click. "Lovely to talk to you too, Jordan." *Who the hell was there with him? Since he didn't want me to know, obviously not Fae. Then...*

She reminded herself that she needed to settle the bill with Maya. She started to write a response to her invoice e-mail when she decided to be more direct and call instead.

"Yes?" Maya's voice sounded very suspicious.

"Hey, Maya, it's Kat."

"Oh. Hey."

# THE FALL OF BLACKSTONE MANSION

"I'm calling to warn you that you're not getting paid through the trust—"

"What? Why not? I did the work!"

"No, no, no. I don't mean you're not gonna get paid at all. I just mean that the funds aren't coming from the trust. They're coming from me personally. I wanted to let you know, so it didn't look fishy."

"Oh. Okay."

"Same as when we go back to finish the plan."

There was a brief pause. "I'm not going back."

"Why not?"

"I'm sending you the files, so you have them."

"I don't understand."

"Ya know, I don't know what freaks me out more, that we heard those moans, felt that chill, smelled that awful whatever it was, that you dragged me out, or that none of that, *none* of it seems to bother you."

*Compared with what I've experienced...* "Is there anything I can say that'll change your mind?"

"There's something wrong with that house. Something very wrong. That you aren't running for the hills blows my mind."

*I can't just leave them, Maya. I have to figure out what happened there.* She didn't know what to say. "I understand."

"I gotta go. I'll send you the files."

"Thanks."

The line clicked.

# AUGUSTINE PIERCE

*I have a partial floor plan, and all it tells me is that a chunk of the house is inaccessible.* "I've gotta go back." *But first, I've got this other crap to take care of. Otherwise, Jordan'll rip me a new one.*

*Who was with him?*

She searched for Portland-area restaurants that had five stars, catered, and just to screw with Jordan, all had four dollar signs. The list was disappointingly short. She zeroed in on three: French, Japanese, and an Argentinian steakhouse. "Probably can't do Japanese for Thanksgiving." She wasn't sure about the French either, but figured it was close enough if necessary. She called the French restaurant, La Muse, first.

"How many people?" an energetic-sounding man asked.

"I'm actually not sure. As few as ten. As many as fifty?" she estimated.

"Pretty wide range."

"I'll have a final count soon." A lie. She had no idea when she'd have a final count if she'd ever have one. *You should ask Fae how she handled the Halloween party.* Then she remembered the confrontation with Fae in the bathroom at Portland City Grill. *Yeah, she's not gonna talk to me except possibly to remind me of how not as hip as her I am.*

"It'll be two hundred a head with a minimum of twenty," the man said. "We'll need at least a week's notice. Better if more."

"Got it. How soon can one of you come and check out the space?"

"Where's the venue located?"

Because she lacked what she felt was a straight-forward, traditional address, she gave him detailed instructions on how to reach the mansion.

"That's *way* out there!" he said.

*If I had a nickel...* "Yeah. Blackstone's way out here."

"Um, we can maybe get someone out tomorrow afternoon. Say, 2:00?"

"That's fine for me."

"I or someone else'll give you a ring tomorrow morning to confirm."

"Great. Thanks." She hung up. The Argentinian restaurant gave her similar numbers, but they couldn't send anyone to check out the mansion until Monday.

---

Katherine sat in her car at the corner of the block next to Jordan's condo tower. She had a direct sight line on the building's entrance so she could see anyone who came and went. Many people had in the hours she'd been sitting here, but none of them wore long black trench coats or wide-brimmed hats. She only felt hesitant when she saw a white van with tinted windows parked in front of the entrance on the Vista's side. The van's plain appearance and lack of activity made her uneasy.

"Come on, come on," she grumbled. "Something. Anything. He had *someone* with him."

*Buzz!* Her phone throbbed in her pocket. She awkwardly extracted it to see that it was Kirk calling. "Hey," she greeted him.

"Hey. Where are ya?"

"The Pearl. Where are you?"

"Just got home."

"Already? It's only..."

"Five thirty."

"Wow. Didn't realize so much time had gone by."

"How long you been up there?"

"A while."

"What're you doin'?"

"Looking for someone."

"Who?"

"That man in black."

"Wait. You mean the same one you saw—?"

"Yeah."

"What makes you think you'll find him up there?"

"Because I'm sure I saw him last Friday when we were out with Jordan and Fae and today, over the phone, Jordan clearly had company, but when I asked him about it, he vehemently denied it."

"I dunno, Kat. Sounds pretty circumstantial."

"Call it a hunch."

"Why didn't you tell me you saw him on Friday?"

"Because I didn't wanna... I didn't wanna... I dunno."

He sounded hurt. "Okay. Well, when're you comin' back?"

"I guess I can—"

The Vista's front entrance opened and out walked not one, but ten men in black. They wore identical outfits, the coats, sunglasses, and hats, but they were different heights, with the tallest about six inches taller than the shortest.

"Oh my God," Katherine said.

The tallest one looked familiar—as much as he could among his peers. She suspected he was the one she'd already seen at Blackstone's town square and at the mansion.

"What? What happened?" Kirk asked.

"It's him—them."

"Wow. How many?"

"I gotta go. I'll see you in a bit."

"Okay. Yeah. See you."

She hung up and waited while the men in black piled into the white van. It headed south, but immediately took a left.

## AUGUSTINE PIERCE

She followed, though wasn't sure how close she should trail them. They'd been sneaky enough not only to spy on her, but also locate her hospital room, so chances were, they were much better at this little game than she was.

Turning left, she saw the van at the end of the block. It made a hard right.

*Do they know I'm after them? Yeah, probably do.* Reaching the end of the block, she took the right, but once she'd finished her turn, she barely caught the van as it had already finished another left turn. *I'm gonna lose 'em!*

With her next turn, she no longer saw any sign of the van. They'd ditched her in only three blocks.

"Damn it!" She slapped her steering wheel. *Great. Now that they know I'm onto them, they'll stay even more hidden.* "Guess I'd better get back."

Arriving at Kirk's place, she found him kind and attentive, but distant. She was sure it was because of her having admitted that she hadn't told him about the previous man-in-black sighting. She knew it was only the latest in her habit of not being open and honest with him. What he didn't understand, though, was that with most things that she didn't share, it wasn't because she didn't want to, but that she didn't know how.

*Jordan's working with the men in black?* What did that even mean? Did he know about the roses sent to her hospital room? Did he order them? No, that didn't seem like him. Too conniving. Too clever.

She and Kirk had a quiet dinner, during which they hardly talked. They went to bed, made love, during which she kept thinking about her men-in-black chase and all its implications. Then they passed out.

---

Katherine stood in the center of the mansion's carriage loop, her eyes locked on the front doors. She was torn. Only yesterday, a spirit, likely Vernon's, had come after her and Maya. But Katherine needed to know what lay at the center of the house. She *needed* to know.

*What can they do to me? Anything other than what they've already done? Send me visions?* She walked slowly toward the front doors and reached her hand out to the right doorknob. She thought of warning the spirits again, like she had weeks ago after Jordan had given her permission to enter the property. On that occasion at least, she'd had the confidence of official family permission.

Her fingertips hung on the doorknob's cold brass. *Maybe I should wait. Ask Kirk to come with me. No. He'd have questions and concerns.*

Her hand lifted from the knob. *I should just go.* "And do what? Hang out at Kirk's all day?"

Her eyes dropped to her purse. She unzipped it enough to see the tiniest hint of the pendant's black. *I should go in.* Before she believed she'd actually decided, she felt that cold brass under her fingers again. She turned the knob and shoved the door open.

Stepping inside, she took out her flashlight and clicked it on. She opened her mouth to inform the spirits as to her intentions, but said nothing. *What's it matter? They'll either come after me or they won't.* She shone her light all around. To her surprise, she easily saw shadows flicker in and out of the beam. She tried to count them, but they were so skittish that it was impossible to tell when one ended and the next began. *What are they doing? Why don't they just come out?* "Got somethin' to say or what?"

No noises sprang from the darkness.

She ignored the shadows and set about doing what she came here to do. She took out her phone and tapped into her files folder. Maya had sent the floor plan, notes, and measurements shortly before Katherine had left Kirk's yesterday. In anticipation of the hill's lack of signal, she'd downloaded them.

She opened one file to see what of the information she could use. It was a list of various measurements. "Might as well be Romanian." As with the language with which she was minimally familiar, she could pick out details, but any overall picture? Impossible.

She opened another file and was relieved to see the image in the style of a pencil sketch. *A map.* Maya had drawn a thick line at the north and south sides of the central area of the house, which they couldn't enter. She'd even circled the area and labeled it "inaccessible." Despite the circle, the east and west sides remained a mystery.

"Start in the right corridor." Katherine referred to the one that connected the east and north towers. "Maybe exactly at the east tower. Walk to the south end of the inaccessible area. Go another, say, two or three doors. Pick one of those. Go left. Toward the area. Keep opening rooms till you hit a dead end."

Satisfied that she had a plan, she put her phone away and walked to her starting point. As she passed through the three hallways to get there, the shadows danced around in her flashlight's beam. None let out a groan or manifested into a full corpse-ghost as both Eileen's and Vernon's had done so many times before. *What are they doing?* Katherine kept thinking of addressing them, but didn't know what to say.

She opened the first door and stepped into the room. There was a door on its other side. She passed through to the next. That one also had a door leading closer to the center. Going through that third one, though, revealed a dead-end room. She saw no seams, symbols, or any other sign that there was any way through.

She nodded. "Okay." Pressing her ear against the blank wall, she heard empty nothingness on the other side. She did not hear any groans or other noises indicating lingering spirits.

She continued north through more rooms that bordered the east side of the central area. Each one looked just like the first, with no sign of how to reach the center. She reached about where the north side met the east side, as shown on Maya's map. The very next room she entered had a door on the west wall.

"Only one more side. If there's no way to get in over there..." She reached for the west wall's door, only to realize she wasn't sure if that was west or east. She turned around to face the opposite door and found she was completely disoriented. She took out her phone and checked Maya's map. It looked like she stood only two or three rooms away from the north tower. If she could get there, she'd be fine.

She exited the current room through what she thought was the east door. That led to a triangular room with a long east side. "This should open into the eastern corridor, between the north and east towers." She stepped out of the room and was deliriously grateful to find herself in a wide corridor. "Now I should be able to go left." She followed her own instruction and soon reached the very familiar north tower entrance.

"All right," she declared as she faced directly south, toward the corner at which the west and east hallways met at a forty-five-degree angle. "Now I just go"—she looked to her right, down the west hallway—"that way."

She hiked to a place farther down at which the map showed that, were she to turn left, toward the east, those rooms would butt up against the central area. She resumed her search as she'd done on the other side.

Every room that bordered the central inaccessible area turned out the same. None had doors that opened into it. None had any other feature that even resembled such an entry point. No seams, no symbols, no switches.

"It's a big, closed-in box," she confirmed to herself in the last possible room that could have granted access. "There has to be some clue, some sign how to get in there." She thought about the various places she'd been in the mansion. The towers, the tombs, the music room, the dining room. The only one that seemed like it would contain any likely answers was the one in which she'd located the pendant, the library at the base of the north tower. She marched back there, determined to find something, any scrap of information that would help her solve this mystery.

She entered the space with bold determination, swinging its doors open wide. She threw her flashlight's beam over to the sliding bookshelf. She didn't open it, however, stopping a few feet short. *Something's off.* She shone her light all around the bookshelf's perimeter, lingering a few seconds on the lever that slid the shelf away from the private study behind. *Oh no.* She could have sworn she saw a fresh set of fingerprints encircling the lever. She thought for a second that she was being paranoid, obsessive, seeing things that weren't really there. Then she lowered her beam to the floor.

Footprints.

Clearly not her own and unless Kirk had visited without her knowing, not his either. That meant someone else, a man, had visited since she'd last stopped by.

She lifted her eyes suspiciously to the lever. She pulled it slowly, half expecting the owner of those footprints to jump out at her.

The shelf slid away. No one jumped out. The space beyond was just as dark and dusty as it had been the last time she'd set foot in it.

Something was off, though. Something she couldn't put her finger on for several seconds. She lifted her flashlight to scan the space. The area directly in front of her felt more open, even cleaner.

The cobwebs were gone.

While her presence here, and Kirk's after that, had likely brushed some aside, there was no way either of their movement cleared away all of them. Then, as her light's beam drifted across the bookcases, and finally onto the little desk, she saw the source of the missing cobwebs, the footprints outside, and the fingerprints on the lever.

Everything was gone.

Every book, every paper on the desk, even the ridiculously expensive black Mason dip pen. All of it. Since her last visit to this study, someone had stripped the entire room clean.

13

Katherine burst into Kirk's apartment, her mind racing. She'd spent the entire drive back from the mansion thinking about the stripped study. *Who took all its articles? Why?* The only reasonable answer was Jordan. Or the men in black acting on his orders. But how did he even know about the study in the first place? Or did they know and tell him?

"Great-grandfather Silas's notes." Those were among Marcus's parting words to his dying brother, Reginald. The Realm and the Formula. Assuming that the study was Silas's, were Jordan and the men in black looking for what Marcus had found over a century ago? Did the volumes on the study's shelves hold all the answers? Did Jordan and the men in black think they did?

*The pendant.* In her haste to understand the removal of the study's books, she'd forgotten about the piece she'd kept on her person since she'd discovered the dusty old chamber. She placed a protective hand over her purse and pressed her fingers into the cloth until she felt the hard edge of the trinket's bars. She sighed with relief, as if her momentary lack of attention on the purse and the pendant inside had somehow put the latter in danger. *I found it in the study. In that safe. Does that mean Jordan was looking for it?* She stroked the edge of the pendant through the purse's cloth. *He can't have it!*

She froze, that last thought having caught her completely off guard. "Okay, Kat, calm down. No one's... We've gotta focus on the issue at hand."

She tried to focus on what was more important right now. "Let's assume he was looking for the pendant. He's not a jewelry guy, so what's so special about it? And he knew I've likely been all over that house, so why didn't he just ask me?" *He doesn't want me to know!* The second she thought it, she knew it was most likely true. *What is Jordan hiding from me? And why even hide? I'm his employee. What does he care what I know or don't know? Am I a threat? If so, why make me his stupid director?*

She shook her head, needing to refocus. "Okay, assuming he wanted the pendant, but didn't find it, why take everything else out? Was there something in those books and papers he wanted, and more importantly, didn't want me to see?"

The books and papers. Where could he have put them? *Not his condo. Too personal. Too easy to misplace or damage them.*

"His law firm?" For the moment, it seemed as good an option as any. She took out her phone, jumped into her e-mail, and looked for the name of the firm to which she'd sent Maya's invoice. Griffin+Miller. She found them in the same fashionable part of northwest Portland where Jordan's condo was. "Time for a drive."

---

"I'm sorry, who are you again?" the blonde woman wearing thick-rim glasses asked from behind the reception desk at the law offices of Griffin+Miller.

"Katherine Norrington. I'm the director of the Blackstone trust."

"Uh-huh..." Ms. Thick-Rim sounded so suspicious, Katherine half expected her next call to be to building security.

"The appointment was recent, but there must be some record of me."

"Checking." Ms. Thick-Rim raised harsh eyebrows. Her expression seemed to say "One more word out of you, missy, and I *will* call security."
"With a K or a C?"

"A K."

"Norrington as in...?"

# THE FALL OF BLACKSTONE MANSION

*As in, come on, lady!* "Usual way. N-O-R-R-I-N-G-T-O-N."

"Hm. Yes, Ms. Norrington. My apologies. I do see you listed." She looked up from her screen. "What was it you needed?"

"You keep items for your clients?"

"Yes."

"I know wills and tax records and stuff like that, but also other kinds of items?"

"What kind do you mean?"

*I don't wanna tell her "old books," or "pendants fashioned in the shape of obscure occult symbols."* "Is it possible that Mr. Blackstone might've dropped things by here, say, for safekeeping?"

"Not that I'm aware of."

*Damn it!*

Ms. Thick-Rim continued, "But the partners don't tell me every detail of every client's affairs."

"Of course. I understand. And as I'm sure you're aware, Mr. Blackstone can be... trying."

Ms. Thick-Rim allowed a tiny smirk, but dared not say anything besmirching a client.

"If Mr. Blackstone did leave anything here, where might I, the director of his trust, check?" Katherine asked.

"We have a room reserved for Mr. Blackstone's affairs."

*Just one room?*

"Would you like to look in there?" Ms. Thick-Rim asked.

"That would be fantastic, yes."

"Please follow me." She stood and led Katherine down a long hallway to a room locked with a keypad. She punched in a code. The door beeped. She opened it for Katherine. "It's all yours."

"Thanks." Katherine found a room full of bookcases packed with binders, several sets of filing cabinets and drawers, and a PC that looked several years old. She waited until Ms. Thick-Rim had closed the door before she started snooping.

She walked over to the nearest set of binders and cracked one open. It was rife with financial data from years ago. "Not gonna be in any tax record." She put the binder back and looked around for any obvious place where someone might have put the mansion's books and papers. Even if Jordan wasn't concerned with his property's things, she guessed his attorneys knew enough to treat delicate articles with care.

She spotted a set of drawers on the other side of the room, opposite the PC. She opened the nearest one. More mundane documents having nothing to do with the mansion's books.

She eyed the PC. "Someone must've tracked the stuff as it came in." She sat and jostled the mouse. The screen lit up with a password prompt. "Crap."

# THE FALL OF BLACKSTONE MANSION

She had no clue what either the firm or Jordan would have used.

She gave it a go with the only clue she had. She typed "Ibiza." The Balearic island in Spain was the one place Jordan had mentioned as a point of pride, having been the location for his first headlining DJ gig.

The password box vibrated and now displayed a message in red...

```
Three more failed attempts before lockout.
```

"Great." She sat back in the chair and sighed. She couldn't risk getting locked out, but also didn't want to leave empty-handed.

The keypad *beeped*.

Her eyes darted to the door as it *clicked* open.

A tall, handsome man with salt and pepper hair stood in the doorway. "Ms. Norrington?"

Katherine stood with a stiffness, as if he'd caught her spying on him. "Yeah?"

"Joel Griffin. Managing partner." He offered his hand.

She shook hands and forced a smile. "Hey."

"I've heard a lot about you."

"At least some good, I hope."

He grinned, but it was flat, as if he wanted to say "No, not really." "Madeline tells me you needed something in Mr. Blackstone's archives."

"Yes. Do you guys have a record of articles removed from the mansion recently?"

"What sort of articles?"

"Books mostly, some papers, and also this really fancy antique pen."

He squinted. "What did you need with these articles?"

*Does that mean he's seen them or not?* She didn't have a great reason for asking about them, so tried the usual route. "My initial association with Mr. Blackstone was to sell the mansion's antiques. Those articles would be part of such an ongoing sale."

Joel continued to stare at her.

"I looked around, but didn't see them in here," she said.

He offered nothing.

"Is there some other place I should be looking?" she asked.

"The only other location I'm aware of is Mr. Blackstone's personal safe deposit box."

"Great! How do I access that?"

"You don't."

"But I'm his director."

"It's his *personal* box. Only he has access."

*Wonderful. Another dead end. Well, since I'm not gettin' anywhere here, might as well go back to Kirk's and... I dunno.* "I understand. Please, pardon my intrusion."

"Not at all, Ms. Norrington. I'll walk you out."

# THE FALL OF BLACKSTONE MANSION

He escorted her to reception, where they exchanged parting pleasantries.

"If you ever need anything else, please don't hesitate to ring ahead." His tone was polite, but carried an admonishing edge. He returned to his office.

Katherine was about to go when she figured she'd make one last attempt. "Madeline, right?"

Madeline stopped typing. "How can I help you, Ms. Norrington?"

Katherine leaned in and spoke in a low tone. "Kat, please."

"All right, Kat."

"How acquainted with Jordan's affairs are you?"

"Not sure what you mean."

"If something comes in on his behalf, does it pass through your hands?"

"Depends. I've seen restaurant bills, hotel bills, that sort of thing all the time."

"Have you seen anything in, say, the last two weeks that caught your eye?"

"Not that I recall, sorry."

*So much for that.* "That's fine."

"Something did come through that I wasn't allowed to see."

"Weren't allowed?"

"A few boxes marked 'fragile.'"

"How many?"

Madeline shook her head. "A dozen? I'm not sure. Why?"

*A dozen fragile boxes could've been the books and papers. But without access to the safe deposit box...* "Nothing. Just trying to figure something out. If you don't mind my asking, how often are you not allowed to see or even know about something that comes in for Jordan?"

"This was the first time."

Katherine nodded. "Thanks, Madeline."

---

Katherine dragged her index finger along the shiny platinum vein. Her gesture was more focused than a mere caress, her fingertip pressing into the metal. The first few times she'd touched the pendant this way, she'd felt a relieved satisfaction. Now, though, each time she touched the piece, she felt a distinct pleasure. It was also a pleasure she couldn't identify. It bore no resemblance to the ones she was used to: sexual, sweetness, pride. But it was a pleasure she increasingly desired.

She was sitting on Kirk's couch, holding the pendant right in front of her eyes. She'd sat like this, with the black-and-platinum item in her hands since she'd arrived hours ago.

# THE FALL OF BLACKSTONE MANSION

*Put it on*, her inner voice commanded. The pendant, while not fashioned in the design of any traditional necklace, had an attached silver chain. The piece screamed to be worn. It was an impulse she'd been fighting to ignore since she first laid eyes on it.

Yet she'd resisted. She couldn't tell why, but just as strong as her urge sometimes was to hang it from her neck, she had a stronger instinct that she should absolutely not do that. The latter feeling persisted, but she could tell, as with her increased pleasure at merely touching the piece, one day she wouldn't be able to fight it anymore, and despite her deepest misgivings about wearing it, she would eventually cave.

She let out a gasping sigh as her fingertip reached the circle attached to the pendant's V-shaped bottom point. The quick strokes across the pendant's five connecting bars elicited spurts of pleasure, but running her finger from its top to bottom, those were by far the most satisfying.

Keys *clinked*. A knob turned. A door opened. While she heard the sounds, she hadn't registered them. They might as well have occurred in some distant realm in her imagination.

"Hey," Kirk said.

The pendant dropped from sight as Katherine's startled hands released it. "Damn it!" Her eyes snapped to her lap. A wave of intense relief washed over her body as she saw the black metal resting on her legs. She seized the piece and tried to shove it back into her purse. Still feeling the remnants of the adrenaline surge, her fingers weren't as nimble as normal and it took two attempts before she could do so.

She zipped the purse and patted it firmly against the seat of the couch. She looked up at him. "Hey." Her voice sounded rushed, as if she'd just hidden a secret lover in the closet so Kirk wouldn't discover him.

Kirk's eyes fell to the purse, and he regarded her curiously for a second, but said nothing. He was probably still trigger shy from the last time he'd dared ask anything about the pendant. "Been back a while?"

"Uh, yeah." She shifted awkwardly, as if her very presence on the couch could telegraph the fact that she'd just spent hours sitting here stroking the pendant.

He sat next to her. He was quiet. Every time they'd greeted each other during weekday evenings since she'd moved in, he'd asked her how her day was. Not now. His eyes glanced across the room at nothing in particular. Something was off. Way off.

She skimmed recent memories to see if there was anything she'd done or said that might have bothered him, which he hadn't already mentioned. Other than the question of when Jordan would take care of his family's remains, she drew a blank. Whatever this was, it wasn't related to her and was very recent.

Still keeping his eyes on nothing in particular, Kirk finally spoke. "How married are you to San Francisco?"

"Why?" She exhaled, relieved that he hadn't mentioned her obvious obsession with the pendant.

His eyes fell to his lap. He hadn't yet looked at her.

*Great. Is he actually hiding a secret lover?*

"Jordan called." Kirk's eyes met hers.

"Really?"

"Yeah."

"What did he say?"

"Remember how he'd mentioned hooking me up with his label?"

"Yeah?"

"Days ago, he'd requested demo tapes or files or whatever."

"He called you days ago?"

"No, this was over e-mail."

"Oh. You never told me."

He shrugged. "Never came up. Anyway, I sent some files over, just, like, three of me in sessions, one live, and he called today."

"And? Don't leave me hanging!"

"I guess his people liked them 'cause they want me to fly out to LA next week and New York the week after to fill in on sessions."

"Wait." She laughed with pride. "Are you telling me, Kirk Whitehead, that you're a professional drummer?"

"I mean, looks like it."

"Through my boss Silver Spoon Baby?"

He shrugged. "Yeah. Pretty nuts."

"So, what's the bad news?"

"What do you mean?"

"The way you came in, you looked like you had bad news."

"Well, depending on how these sessions go, how other things go, I don't know that I can move to San Francisco with you."

She leaned back on the couch. Suddenly, this conversation felt very different, almost like high school sweethearts discussing what would happen when they went to separate colleges. "With me?" Those were the words she spoke, but what she wanted to ask was "Are you dumping me?"

"The way you were talking Sunday sounded like you were set on us moving to San Francisco."

"Or LA or wherever!"

"Right."

"So..."

"Kat, don't get me wrong. I wanna go where you wanna go. I'm just not sure where I should be if this thing with Jordan's label works out."

"Does it matter?"

"Where I am?"

"Yeah."

"I mean, that's the thing. I don't know where I should be."

"Since you wanna be available for sessions and don't wanna fly across the country every time, probably LA."

"I guess so. That okay?"

"LA?"

"Yeah."

"Sure! I love me some beach and Walk of Fame."

He grinned with relief. "Great, then I guess LA it is. Maybe in two weeks?"

"Maybe." She put her leg over his. "I think we should sleep on it."

He smiled wide. "After you."

## 14

Katherine's phone rang with a number that looked familiar, but she couldn't recall. At least it wasn't Jordan. Then again, it already being 9:30 in the morning, it was far too late for him to bother her.

"Hello?" she asked the caller.

"Ms. Norrington?" a familiar, energetic male voice asked.

"Speaking."

"Hey, it's Arnold calling from La Muse in Portland."

*La Muse... La Muse...*

Her hesitation must have been noticeable, as he then clarified. "You were interested in catering services for Thanksgiving?"

*The French place!* "Right! Yes! That was today."

"Unless today doesn't work."

"No, no, no. Today's good. What time?"

"I was gonna be out there by two, if that still works."

"Yeah. Great. No problem. I will be there..."

"Arnold."

"Wonderful, Arnold. Thanks for confirming. Oh, and please keep in mind that cell coverage is nonexistent on the hill."

"Duly noted."

"And you may wanna bring a flashlight."

"Gotcha. See you in a bit."

---

"Hey, you're back," Stacey greeted Katherine from inside the mansion's gate as the latter dodged PGE workers.

For the first time since meeting her, Katherine detected a note of suspicion in the younger woman's voice. She trod cautiously. "Here to show a caterer around."

Approaching them, Jordan's face lit up. "Finally, some good news! Who'd we go with?"

"Well, there's more than one," Katherine said. "The place visiting today is La Muse. Monday is this Argentinian steakhouse, El Toro."

"La Muse... Isn't that the really fancy French place?"

"Yeah. I haven't been there."

"French isn't exactly Thanksgiving fare."

"Neither is Argentinian."

"Right, so, shouldn't you, o director, find someone who is?"

"Unfortunately, these two and a Japanese place were the highest rated in the city. Unless you wanna skimp on quality..."

"I like Japanese," Stacey contributed.

Both Katherine and Jordan ignored her.

"No, no. That's fine," he said. "Just not sure what French turkey's gonna be like."

"Probably a lot like American," Katherine said.

"Yeah." His mind seemed to wander. "Yeah, whatever you go with, I'm sure it'll be fine. I'll leave you to it."

*Huh. He wasn't nearly as upset as I thought he'd be. Maybe turning a new leaf?* "All right. Good luck with the electrical stuff." She started up the hill.

"Oh, Kat?"

She turned around.

He took a few steps toward her before continuing in a hushed tone. "Next time you wanna go snooping around my firm, just tell me what you're looking for and I'll hook you up."

*How did he know? Madeline. She totally snitched on me even after our little bonding session over how irritating he is! Or are the men in black still watching me? Probably are. But to what end?* "Uh, yeah. No problem."

"What *were* you looking for?" Jordan's tone sounded far more suspicious than she was expecting.

*What's he hiding? Something big? Come on, Jordan! Drop a hint!* She wasn't sure how to respond. If she outright lied and he caught her, he'd likely fire her and bar her from ever setting foot on the property again. She'd never uncover the mansion's remaining secrets. Never discover the true nature of the pendant. Never understand why Marcus murdered his family. But if she told Jordan the truth, he'd probably ask her even more probing questions she didn't want to answer. "Just some books and things."

"Books?"

"Yeah. I found a library or study and books can be really valuable to the right collectors."

He nodded, seeming to like where this was going.

"Some seemed to be missing," she continued, "and I was concerned that without the entire collection, the room wouldn't be worth as much."

He nodded again, seeming to be satisfied with her answer. "You could've called me." He sounded intensely relieved, as if he, too, had dodged a bullet.

"Didn't wanna bother you with it."

"I understand. Well, best leave you to helping out that caterer."

"Yeah." *Thank God that's over with!* She again started up the hill.

"Oh, Kat?"

She faced him.

"That study?" he asked.

"Yeah?"

"Something does seem to be missing from it."

"Oh?" Her adrenaline surged. *Great. I'm caught. Well, here goes getting kicked off the property.*

"Yeah. My great-whatever grandfather's notes mention a... Well, I'm not exactly sure what to call it."

*Great-grandfather? You mean Marcus?*

"Some sort of trinket or necklace or something. Doesn't ring any bells, does it?"

*Great. I can't tell him about the pendant! It's mine! I found it! He can't have it! Whoa, Kat. Do* not *say that! Well, guess I do gotta lie now!* "No."

"Not at all?"

"No, sorry." She shook her head for emphasis.

"It's just when we collected those books..."

*"We"? Who's we? You and your lawyers? You and the men in black? You and your lawyers* and *the men in black?*

He continued, "We found a safe. Opened. Empty. The same dimensions my grandfather described."

*Damn it, Kat! Why didn't you close the stupid safe?*

"Still not ringing any bells?"

"Sorry, Jordan. No."

"The keys used to open the safe? The amount of dust on them? Shows they were used recently."

"Very interesting."

"If I were to send those keys to a specialist, I wonder whose prints would show up."

# THE FALL OF BLACKSTONE MANSION

*Dead to rights.* "Has anyone else besides me and you been in there?"

He stared at her a second, then cast his eyes aside, as if someone else did pop into his head. "No."

*Who's he thinking of? The men in black? Just say it, Jordan! You're working with them to some nefarious end!* With his brief distraction, she attempted to extract some answers out of him. "Oh, Jordan?"

"Yeah?"

"Your family's remains."

He took another step toward her. His tone darkened. "Kat, I told you not to—"

She took a defiant step toward him, breaching his personal space. "I was there. I found them. They're human bodies. Murdered. I could be held liable." She chose not to complicate the matter by mentioning Kirk's also having been present.

"That won't happen."

"All the county has to do is—"

"I've made arrangements with the county."

"Jordan, just lay them to rest in their frickin' graves in your family's personal, private cemetery!" She pointed in its direction.

He stepped back. His tone and expression both softened. He averted his gaze. "I prefer to keep all the bodies where they were buried. Call it family tradition."

*"All" the bodies? He put Gloria back in her tomb too?*
"I... I don't..."

"I'll let you get to that caterer." He turned around and marched back to Stacey without another word.

*What was that all about?* For the moment, how he handled his dead relatives' remains was the least of her concerns. With his notion of lifting prints from the safe keys, she now had a target on her back. If he ordered such a procedure today, he'd likely get the results back in less than a week. Whatever she was going to do, she needed to do it now.

She headed for the mansion's entrance. She paused at the doors and gazed up at the front of the building, all the way to the top of its conical roof. *I have no more clue than I did days ago when Maya and I arrived. Guess I'm just gonna have to...* She opened the right door and stepped inside.

## 15

Katherine clicked on her flashlight and shone it on Artemis's face. Katherine saw no flitting shadows crossing the beam as she studied the statue's still features, the curves of its cheekbones. "If I'm a Blackstone and I wanna have access to a room or section of my mansion, but I don't want it to be obvious, what do I do? Where do I put it?"

She took out her phone and checked the map Maya had sent. *That middle area.* There had been no access to it through any of the adjacent rooms. There was also no other way in that she'd so far seen. No doors. No stairways.

She looked back up at Artemis. "I don't want it to be obvious, but it's gotta be easy enough that I can get at it whenever I need." She directed her beam to Apollo's face. "It's not gonna be in a room I use every day. Not the dining room. Not the master. Not gonna be where curious kids can go reaching for it. But it's also not gonna be in the most obscure corner of the house. I've gotta be able to just walk to it. Not too many stairs. Not too many corners. Probably the first floor. Not too deep into the house."

*The study in the north tower?* The choice only seemed likely because that was where she'd found both the pendant and the entrance to the final tomb. Two giant discoveries waiting in one location.

She checked the time. She still had an hour before Arnold from La Muse arrived to size up the kitchen. "Guess if I don't find it by then, I can get him set up, keep searching."

She worked her way through the hallways to the north tower. She opened its left door and slipped inside. Now that she was looking for some kind of switch, she felt like she had to be a little more careful in here than she had before.

She cast her beam around the room. The bookshelves looked as they always had. Rows upon rows of dusty spines. She saw nothing that looked even the slightest bit suspicious. "Not too obvious, but easy enough." Already feeling defeated, she pointed her flashlight at the sliding bookshelf. "Maybe I missed something in there."

She gripped the steel lever and pulled the bookshelf away from the opening to the hidden study. She shone her light inside. While she'd only seen this half of the room twice when it was full of books and papers, the space still struck her as distinctly disconcerting now that it lacked them. *At least it helps with searching for hidden switches.*

She scoured every inch of the desk, the flat wall above it with the open safe, and the semicircular wall where the now-empty bookcases stood.

Absolutely nothing.

She sighed. "Okay, Kat, it's not gonna be, like, a button. It's gonna be..." No other possibilities leapt into her head. To be extra thorough, she shone her flashlight along every edge in the room, hoping for some clear sign of construction, like the seams she'd discovered in the other towers' walls.

Only infuriatingly flawless stonework.

"All right," she told herself. "All right!" she repeated to the room. "Fine. I guess it's not in here."

She headed for the mansion's entrance without even bothering to close either the sliding bookshelf or the tower's door. *Gonna have to regroup. Re-think this. If only I had access to Marcus's notes! They probably say exactly where the central area's entrance is!*

She stopped when she realized she did not know where she was. She couldn't even remember which hallway she'd taken from the north tower. *Great. Eh, just keep going till you run into some other tower.*

In a few more seconds, she arrived at a tower's entrance. She threw her beam down the opposite hallway. *So is this...?*

She froze when the hazy left edge of the flashlight beam's circle illuminated the nose and chin of Silas's bust. *Oh my God. Could it be that obvious?* She walked down the rest of the main west-east hallway and parked in front of the austere old man's black marble face. "Has it been you the entire time?" She tried not to get too excited, but the more she thought about it, the more it made sense. This statue wasn't only a physical symbol of Silas's ego, it was the literal centerpiece of the whole mansion.

"Slow down, Kat. Assuming you're right, still gotta crack the code." She shone her light point-blank into the bust's face and studied the sculptor's work. While no art expert, she'd visited enough museums and seen enough private collections to know that this head boasted as fine of work as any masterpieces. There were no seams or blemishes of any kind.

She leaned in for a closer look and inspected the eyes, nose, mouth, and chin. The eyes didn't seem like she could push them into their sockets. The nose had no joint at which she could twist it up. She shone her light on both ears, but saw no sign of any kind of mechanism.

She stood up straight and sighed. *Maybe I was wrong. Maybe it's just a bust. Was only a hunch, anyway.* She lowered her flashlight's beam to where the neck met the floor of the niche.

## THE FALL OF BLACKSTONE MANSION

*Wait a sec.* A detail had caught her eye. She got on one knee and leaned in to only a couple of inches away from the bottom of the bust. She traced the line from left to right where the neck's marble met the niche's wood. "Look at that." The wood didn't disappear under the bust. It curved down where it met the marble. *The head goes* into *the niche!* Scanning across the area of the neck where it met the niche, she also noticed that for about an inch above the point of contact, the marble had no sculpted articulation of Silas's neck. The full bottom inch of the bust was a smooth cylinder.

"Does that mean...?" She stood up straight and regarded the bust with a whole new level of admiration. "That I can push it down?"

She didn't waste another second. Setting her flashlight bottom side up to the right of the bust, she placed both hands on top of the head and pushed down.

She felt immediate and intense resistance, as if she were attempting to rotate a crank that no one had turned in generations. She heard very encouraging sounds emanate from within the wall behind and surrounding the niche. The *groan* of wood sliding against wood and the *clack* of stone and metal components shifting into place.

The bust began to descend.

Biting cold stabbed into her fingertips. That too-familiar rotting stench blasted up her nostrils. Darkness wrapped around her like a heavy black cloak. She even heard the *smack* of her flashlight hitting the floor.

She released the top of the marble head and rubbed her hands together to warm them. That was when she realized she could no longer see the bust, its niche, the hallway, or the floor. Nor her flashlight's dusty beam or the shadows it might have cast.

Vernon's skull thrust into view. Startled, she stepped back. But before she could say or do anything else, his skeletal right hand appeared and his jawbone *cracked* open. His index finger jabbed the air, pointing behind her. A *groan* rang in her ears. It was as loud as the one Eileen's ghost had billowed at her when it first appeared.

"Leave me alone!" Katherine exploded at the specter. She then stepped forward, reached into the black, and slapped her hands down on the top of the bust.

Vernon's ghost and the impenetrable veil it had brought with it both vanished. Katherine could again see highlights of Silas's head under the indirect beam of her flashlight.

She pressed down on the bust. The progress was very slow, but she could feel the marble lower in relation to the niche that contained it. For several seconds, the bust continued to sink. Then it stopped. All movement. All sound.

"What happened?" she asked the niche, and threw a quick glance at its sides, top, and at the surrounding walls.

Nothing had changed.

No secret doors had opened. No levers had appeared. There was no sign that her action had any effect on anything.

"But I felt it! Heard it!" she told the bust.

Silas's face remained silent.

She relaxed her pressure on the top of the head. The marble rose to its initial position.

She stood back and glared at the sculpture. It was so frustrating to have finally made some progress, only to be stumped now. "Something was happening," she reminded the bust.

She cast her glance to the right, down the hallway. At least in the dusty black, there was no reminder of her current failure staring back at her. "Think, Kat. Same guy designed all of this and probably never got that creative."

She thought back on the different versions of the pendant's symbol she'd found in each of the mansion's towers. How in each case, she'd had to push the metal symbols into the wall. "And then slide it in another direction!" she declared to the bust.

She placed her hands on top of the head and pushed it down. The process felt far easier this time, with the wall's internal wooden *groans* seeming to call out sooner and faster. The sculpture reached the bottom of its descent. *All right, Kat, now what?* She'd seen no sign that she could slide the bust in any direction. "But what if I turn it?" She gripped the head by the ears and twisted it to the right.

As with her first attempt at lowering the sculpture, getting it to rotate was no easy task. The marble moved, though, and in another few seconds, she heard an even louder *clack* from behind the walls.

She stepped back from the bust and its niche. With a creaking languidness, the entire section of wall, about a foot in each direction from the niche, revolved to the right, like an ancient hotel entrance.

She swiped her flashlight from off the floor and shone it ahead. A cramped cavity held the niche and its underlying mechanics of clockwork gears and shafts. Between the mechanics and Katherine's feet lay a tight stone corkscrew staircase.

She scanned the exposed section of wall for any sign of a way to return the whole thing back to its former state. To her left, a lever of a similar design to the one that operated the north tower's sliding bookshelf stuck out right next to where the cavity opened up. "Hope that still works."

# THE FALL OF BLACKSTONE MANSION

She pointed her flashlight down into the staircase. Those dark gray steps were so narrow, if she wasn't careful, she could end up tripping all the way. She threw a quick glance down both ends of the hallway as if awaiting permission from Vernon's ghost or some other silent, invisible bystanders.

With a quick, determined breath, she descended the steps. Her flashlight's beam bounced down from the edge of one to the surface of the next. She wondered how far they went. Would they lead to yet another tomb? Some other hidden study? Or something far more disturbing?

She reached flat ground. *Wow, that was fast!* If she had to guess, she figured the descent wasn't even a grand total of six feet.

Before her stretched a narrow, featureless corridor that ended in a doorway-sized opening of bright light. She instinctively pointed her flashlight in that direction, but it revealed nothing. She clicked it off and put it in her purse. *A torch? But no one's come down here in over a century. Besides, the light isn't flickering like a flame. Can't be electric. They're still figuring that out.*

She strode at a quick, though cautious, pace toward the light, arriving in only a few seconds. It turned out to be an opening into a much larger area. When her eyes adjusted, she let out a loud gasp. "What is *that*?"

The long-awaited area was, as Maya had predicted, a huge, cubic space, the size of one-ninth of the mansion's total volume. The ground was stone, much like that which made up the tombs. From its edges rose the mansion's walls, beyond which Katherine and Maya had heard hollow silence. The ceiling was composed of a web of gleaming metal beams that held in place dozens of glass plates. Together, it all resembled the roof of a greenhouse.

But none of that was what had stolen Katherine's breath.

At the dead center stood a tower constructed from jagged, chunky river rocks. It looked like a giant had uprooted a wishing well from the twisted depths of a child's nightmare and stabbed it straight down into the mansion. Attached to the tower's surface a few inches above Katherine's eye level was a version of the pendant's symbol she'd not yet seen in the house. It was complete. An equilateral triangle and intersecting V.

She took slow steps toward the wishing-well tower. She didn't know what to make of any of this. While she'd gotten used to the idea that someone had built the tombs as additions to the house, she never would have guessed what they, the silver bands that seemed to connect them, the floor plan based on the pendant's symbol, and now this tower all clearly showed. Whatever strange, twisted system all these elements comprised... "They weren't built for the mansion. The mansion was built for them."

## 16

Katherine paused halfway between the opening to the mansion's central space and its dominating tower. She unzipped her purse, took out the pendant, and held it up so that it covered her view of the symbol on the tower.

Identical.

She strode the rest of the way to the tower and stared up at its symbol. She held the pendant on top of it to confirm. An exact match. She put the pendant back in her purse and zipped it up. "What's it all for?" She surveyed her surroundings, the mansion's walls, and the stone floor. There was no sign of how any of it was connected.

She walked around the tower. If she were to guess, its circumference was about fourteen feet. Unfortunately, she found no more symbols or any other markings, only blank river rocks. Returning to the spot before the symbol, she studied it some more. *Why's it complete? Why's it the only one in the house that is?* She thought back on the others, one symbol for each tower. Each one had a piece missing, which she'd realized had designated its position in relation to the others.

She thought about how she'd opened the other towers' tombs. She'd had to press each one's symbol into the wall, then move it toward its missing piece. For the west tower to the left, the east tower to the right, and so on. But this tower's symbol had no missing pieces.

She reached up and pressed her hands against it. It didn't budge.

*Not pressing hard enough?* She pushed her hands into the metal so hard it hurt. She stepped away and rubbed her hands. "Not moving. So is it there just for decoration?" Doubting that and remembering how the west and east tombs had entrances built into the walls, but the entryway hall had its built into its staircase, and the north's was built into the floor, she again scanned the surface of this wishing-well tower and the floor surrounding it.

*There!* Directly below the symbol, all around where she was standing, she found clear seams in the stone that looked very much like the pattern that the north tower's tomb entrance had. A descending spiral staircase. *But how do I open it?* She'd seen no obvious mechanism, but given everything she'd experienced in the mansion so far, she reasoned that there had to be a way in. A direct, straight-forward, and even logical one. *Probably not gonna be as obvious as the lever on the other side of that bust.*

*Wait. The bust! How long have I been in here?* She checked her phone. She had about three minutes before the caterer was due to arrive. "Crap!"

She ran back through the tunnel. She clumsily opened her purse and took out her flashlight. Clicking it on, she stumbled up the staircase's steps. Reaching the surface of the familiar west-east hallway, she pulled on the lever next to the wall cavity and stepped back several feet.

With a series of *clicks* and *groans*, the wall section containing the cavity revolved back into its former position, hiding any trace of the staircase. Silas's bust and the niche that contained it were again the only distinct features visible in the hallway.

Katherine nodded at the bust, as if they'd just shared an intimate secret. She then headed outside to find Arnold.

Arriving at the bottom of the hill, she found Stacey still by herself next to the gate. Katherine waved. Stacey waved back.

A van with a painted blue sign that read La Muse pulled up to the gate.

"Who's this?" Stacey pointed to the van.

"Possible caterer for Thanksgiving," Katherine answered. She walked out the gate to greet Arnold as

# THE FALL OF BLACKSTONE MANSION

he got out of the van. He was tall and handsome with short, dark hair.

Stacey's eyebrows leapt to the top of her head. "He can baste my turkey any day!"

Katherine threw her an admonishing glance. *C, he's standing right here!*

"One of you Kat Norrington?" Arnold didn't seem to have heard Stacey's comment.

"I could be." Stacey raised her hand.

"Ignore her. Sorry. Yeah, me." Katherine offered her hand.

"Arnold." He shook hands. "Nice to meet you in person. So, this the site?"

"Yeah, just up the hill." She pointed.

"Let's take a look."

She led him through the gate.

As they passed Stacey, she commented, "If you need any help..."

Katherine shot her another glance. *Shut* up, *C!*

After a few steps, Arnold asked Katherine, "So this is some rich guy's private event?"

"Half right. Jordan is some rich guy, but it's not private."

"But it will be twenty minimum?"

"I wouldn't worry about that. There'll be plenty of people."

"As long as we get an accurate count."

"I will get you that as soon as I can."

They reached the carriage loop before he made any comment on the house.

He lifted his gaze all the way to the roof. "Stunning."

"Yeah. Pretty impressive."

"So the kitchen's…?"

"On the ground floor." She continued up the steps and opened the right door for him. Inside, she took out and clicked on her flashlight.

"Awfully dark."

"Yeah, they're workin' on that now."

"Will everything be turned on in time for Thanksgiving?"

"I really hope so."

"'Cause I dunno that I can ask my staff to work in the dark, even with flashlights."

"No, of course not. I wouldn't expect that." *Though whether Jordan would is a different question.*

She led Arnold to the kitchen and opened the door wide. She made a 180 sweep with her flashlight.

He took out his own and turned it on. Walking around the kitchen's island, he inspected everything from the pots and pans to the cupboard of antique china. "Little smaller than I was expecting, but we can work with it."

"If you need to spill over into nearby rooms, I think that'd be fine."

# THE FALL OF BLACKSTONE MANSION

He faced her. "I doubt that'll be necessary, but it would be nice to discuss it with the owner."

"Let's go see how busy he is."

They soon headed back down the hill. About halfway, they ran into Jordan and a handful of electricians. He was in the middle of grumbling when he spotted them.

"Kat! Who's your friend?" Jordan asked.

"Arnold's the head chef at La Muse, our caterer," Katherine said.

"La Muse. Was that the Argentinian one?"

"No. French."

"Thought I said I preferred Argentinian."

Katherine attempted to ease him a few feet away from the others. He didn't budge. She at least lowered her voice. "No, you didn't. Besides, I thought I was picking the caterer."

"You were. Until you picked French." Jordan then turned to Arnold. "Sorry you came all this way." He continued down the hill with the electricians.

Katherine gave Arnold an embarrassed smile. "One second."

Arnold nodded and trailed after her.

"Jordan," she called.

He ignored her.

"Jordan!" she repeated.

He paused and faced her. "There an issue, Kat?"

She stopped right in front of him so she could at least attempt to keep their conversation between them. "You told me you wanted me to pick—"

"And I *just* told you unless it was—"

"If you wanted Argentinian, why didn't you say that?"

"'Cause I was dealing with the electricity."

"You can't keep undermining every decision I make, otherwise this won't work."

He looked like he was about to counter her, then thought better of it. "Argentinian will be fine."

"You're not gonna change your mind Monday after they've come out here?"

Jordan cast a glance up at poor Arnold, who was still politely waiting for them to figure this out. "I will not." He walked backward. "Have a great, productive weekend." He was most likely referring to the fact that her antique-moving endeavor continued the following morning. He continued with the electricians. "Sorry about that. So, we can or can't make the eighteenth?"

"Actually, Mr. Blackstone, I think we can," an electrician answered.

Katherine sighed. Arnold joined her.

"I'm really sorry," she said. "I didn't know he was gonna do that."

Arnold shrugged, though he looked very annoyed. "It was a pleasant drive."

# THE FALL OF BLACKSTONE MANSION

"I'll walk you to your van."

After Arnold left, Katherine watched Jordan chat with the electricians for another few seconds before joining Stacey. "So I guess I'll see you around."

"Sooner I hope."

"Yeah." Katherine wanted to say more, but decided not to. She got into her car and drove down the hill. She soon slowed. *I've got an idea.*

## 17

The PGE vehicles began to pass by. Katherine watched them from her hidden parking spot a few yards off the road to the mansion. She'd waited here for hours for any sign that the workday was ending, as that meant Jordan would head home. She'd finally get her chance to follow him and see if the men in black showed up.

*There he goes*, she thought at the sight of his Ferrari flying by. She waited till he was a good half minute ahead of her before she drove out of the woods. Hitting the road, she was careful to stay far enough behind him that he wouldn't notice her. She seemed to be pulling it off as he never checked his rearview or in any other way looked suspicious.

*Maybe I should scoot in a little...*

The white van barreled in out of nowhere onto the road behind Jordan.

*Ooh, that was close!* She dropped back a little more from the van, hoping they hadn't yet detected her. She suspected her hope was a vain one as they'd so far proved they could learn anything about her they wanted.

She trailed Jordan and the van onto the highway, past Blackstone and Creek. She guessed they were heading all the way back to his place.

*Kirk!* He'd be home soon and wonder where she was. *Better text him.* She took out her phone, but the moment she started typing, she realized how difficult it would be to keep her eyes on the road at the same time. *No wonder so many text accidents.* She tapped the voice memo app. "Hey, baby, not gonna be home for a while. Tracking Jordan and these creepy guys in black. Hopefully have some good pics for you. See you soon." That parting sentiment was a bit of a lie. It would take over an hour to get to Jordan's neighborhood and thus over an hour to get back. By the time she returned, it'd be close to bedtime.

But she wanted proof. That she wasn't crazy. That the men in black had been following her. That they were working with Jordan. If she didn't do it now, she didn't know the next time she could.

For about twenty minutes, she stayed behind the van and Jordan. She'd seen no change in their driving behavior. Neither vehicle had turned off the highway or made any other move to lead her to believe that they were on to her.

*Buzz!* It was her phone. She lifted it to see that Kirk had sent a message. "Be safe. See you soon." With his blessing, she could relax more into the drive.

The rest of the time to the Pearl flew by. Before she knew it, Jordan and the van had arrived at his building. She panicked, not seeing anywhere nearby to park. She turned off the last street before the Vista and scoured for a spot.

None.

She reached the end of the current block and continued onto the next one. Luckily, she located a paid spot, but she worried that by the time she reached Jordan and the men, they already would have gone inside or somewhere else.

She paid for parking and ran back to the corner of the building opposite the Vista. For once, she was the one hiding in the shadows, spying on them.

There they were. Jordan and the men in black conversing between the van and the building's entrance. Katherine couldn't hear anything distinct, only murmured syllables. She took out her phone and tapped on the camera app. Framing, she found she wasn't able to get a good angle that captured both Jordan and at least one of the men.

She snuck behind a nearby car by the side of its hood. She poked her head and phone out. *Gotcha!* She had Jordan and three of the men in her sights.

# THE FALL OF BLACKSTONE MANSION

*Click!* The area lit up. *Crap!* She'd forgotten to turn off the flash.

All heads turned in her direction. She dove behind the hood and started her clumsily crouched march back toward her car.

Passing the corner, she stood up straight against the wall, her knees sore from having been bent for so many feet. She peeked around the corner.

A shorter man in black was hot on her trail, only a few feet away.

She ran down the street, hoping he wouldn't notice the *slap slap* echo of her shoes against the pavement. Looking back, she saw the man round the corner. She ducked in front of a compact car and squatted against its radiator grill. There she stayed, fighting to control her adrenaline-infused breath.

Distant, determined footsteps.

She fell to her hands and knees, crawling to the car's front-left tire. She peered in the man's direction.

He stood in the middle of the street, only a few yards away, scanning the immediate area. Because of the intensely black shade of his sunglasses, she couldn't see where his eyes wandered.

Seconds dragged by. Her hands and knees started to hurt, but she didn't dare budge for fear of making even the slightest sound that he could then track.

Finally, seemingly satisfied that either she wasn't here or he simply couldn't locate her, he turned around and headed back to the others.

The instant he disappeared beyond the corner onto the street in front of the Vista, she climbed to her feet, and ran to her car. Wincing at the *beep* the unlocking door made, she jumped in, slammed it shut, and fired up the engine.

She checked her rearview. The man had not returned. She got on her way.

---

"There! You see?" Katherine asked Kirk as he stared at the picture on her phone of Jordan and the men in black.

"It's Jordan," Kirk noted.

"And?"

"A bunch of guys dressed as Amish mad scientists."

"Right!"

"So?"

"So it proves that these guys, the same ones who've been stalking me, probably the same ones who sent me those black roses and creepy poem about me and Dean, are working with him!"

"Maybe I'm missing something."

"Nope! It's all right there!"

"No, Kat, I mean, yeah, it proves your suspicion, but what difference does it make?"

"What are you talking about? Now I know!"

"Look, I don't mean to dismiss it, but what does it change? You gonna stop investigating the mansion? Stop working for Jordan?"

"No, of course not."

"Have these men committed a crime?"

"Stalking's a crime."

"A *crime* crime. Have they threatened your life? Have they even gotten close to you?"

She sat next to him on the couch and relieved him of her phone. "No, but..."

"Unless you're gonna call the police and report them, doesn't seem like it changes anything—until they threaten your life."

"I could report it." *But I'm not going to. All they'd have to do is suggest to Jordan that I was the snitch and he could bar me from ever again setting foot on his property.*

"If you want, I can set up a security system. Record all activity around the apartment. If we catch 'em, we can show that to the police."

"No, you're right. It'd only tip 'em off." She sighed. "I guess I just wanted to know."

"I understand."

"For now, I'll keep my eyes peeled. Make sure they don't get too close."

He grinned. "I'll keep 'em away from you." He kissed her, then stood and went to the bedroom.

Remaining on the couch, she opened an image search with the picture. The results almost entirely consisted of Jordan. Many were shots of him on Caribbean beach and Swiss ski trips she'd already seen in her initial research when she'd first found out about him.

As for the men in black, nothing definitive came up. Mostly matching images of either men in traditional Amish hats, models showing off the latest in trench coat fashion, or that of ridiculously expensive, high-end sunglasses.

Beyond that, the internet trail went cold.

Kirk called from the bedroom, "We've got a big day tomorrow."

"That we do." She entered the bedroom and plugged in her phone. Then, sliding under the covers, she nestled into him, and drifted off to uneasy sleep.

## 18

Katherine's index fingertip dragged down the right side of the pendant's V. The gesture was still pleasurable, but not nearly as much as it had been. In fact, she'd noticed lately that in order to derive the same amount of pleasure from interacting with the piece, she'd had to do so more often and with more intensity.

"Kat?" Kirk asked.

"Yeah?"

"Gonna be ready soon?"

"For what?"

"Today."

She looked up to find him fully dressed and ready to go. *Today... today. Oh no! I totally forgot! We're working!* "Yeah." She looked down as if she needed to confirm. She was still in her underwear.

She'd gotten up an hour ago, when she thought he'd still be asleep for a long time, and had come out here to sit on the couch and enjoy her pendant time in peace. She was no longer trying to hide the strange behavior from him, but she was still attempting to find time in which to do it when he wouldn't bother her.

She put the pendant in her purse and zipped it up. When she stood from the couch, she noticed he was regarding her with a very skeptical expression. He looked like he really wanted to ask about what she'd been doing, but he didn't. She guessed he didn't want her to bite his head off over the pendant all over again.

"Just one sec," she said.

"Better hurry."

She ran into the bedroom and threw her clothes on. While she was pulling a sweater over her head, she heard the front door open and close. *He's not gonna make me walk, is he?* Running outside, she found him standing in front of his truck, arms folded, but wearing a relaxed expression. He wasn't quite smiling, but at least he wasn't frowning, either.

*Guess he just wanted to put a little fire under my ass.*

They got going. They were both silent for a minute.

Thinking about today, her mind drifted to... *That central tower. How do I get in? There was no other lever, no switch, but there's gotta be a way!*

"You okay?" he asked.

"Yeah. Why?"

"You're being really quiet."

## THE FALL OF BLACKSTONE MANSION

"Yeah, nothing, just..." She didn't bother finishing the sentence. *What's the logic? The mechanism? Each outer tower has an incomplete representation of the pendant as its symbol, but the central tower has the whole thing.* She went over her memories of opening all the other towers to see if she could come up with any clue she'd somehow missed.

"Kat?" he asked.

"Yeah?"

"We're here." He pointed out the windshield.

The mansion's gate stood right before them. Several trucks had already arrived. The usual crew who'd moved previous rooms' pieces and aided in opening Gloria's tomb all chatted in the street. Shane, Randy, Dennis, Ross, and a few whose names Katherine didn't remember.

"Right. 'Course." She got out, stood near the gate, and pressed her fingers into her purse, stroking the pendant's bars.

Kirk wished the guys good morning and passed out walkie-talkies. One man wearing a goatee and flannel waved to Katherine. Recognizing him, she waved back, but didn't say anything for fear of screwing up his name.

Kirk gave her a walkie-talkie. "Ready to break it down for 'em?"

*I didn't miss anything! There's no way to open the central tower!* "Yeah. Break it down."

"You okay?"

"Yes. I'm fine. Why do you keep asking me that?"

"Sorry. I'll round 'em up."

He walked over to the other guys and signaled for them to join her. They all gathered around.

"'Morning, guys. Um, why don't we mix it up today? Start on the second floor, first room on the right?"

The guys all nodded and grunted their agreement.

"Lunch orders at eleven and all that."

More nods and grunts.

"You heard her. Let's saddle up!" Kirk ordered.

He and the rest of the guys started the hike up the hill. Katherine followed, but made no attempt to keep up with them. When she reached the carriage loop, she found the front doors open. They'd already all gone in.

She paused there and unzipped her purse. Looking down at the pendant, she asked, "What's the connection with the central tower? What's the mechanism?"

The pendant didn't answer.

She zipped up her purse and headed inside. Even though the open doors partly illuminated the entryway hall, she still took out her flashlight and turned it on.

# THE FALL OF BLACKSTONE MANSION

Heading up the staircase, she paused when she caught sight of the symbol on the plaque at the corner where the second floor's two hallways met. This symbol was the one missing its V portion, under which Katherine and Kirk's crew had discovered the entrance to the tomb that had contained Gloria's remains. *Missing its bottom part. Push down and the tomb opens.*

"Joining us?" Kirk waited for her at the top of the staircase.

Katherine climbed the rest of the way. "For a little while."

"We're finishing light setup."

"Sounds good."

He led her into the room where the guys were hard at work. It was a lady's boudoir with particularly elegant chairs and sofas, and bright white walls with yellow accents. It was likely Gloria's private space to entertain friends.

Katherine stood in the corner while Kirk turned on the last of the lights. As he stepped away from it, she threw him a nod.

"What's up?" he asked.

"Do any of these guys have a notepad or scratch paper or, ya know...?"

"Not sure. What for?"

"Nothing huge. Just some ideas I wanted to scribble down."

"Hold on. I'll ask." He made the rounds.

The man who'd earlier waved at Katherine nodded to Kirk. Together, they joined her.

"Mac's got a notebook in his truck," Kirk informed her.

"You got any pens?" Katherine asked.

"Probably," Mac said.

"Could I maybe borrow a pen and a page?"

"Sure thing. I'll go fetch 'em." Mac turned to go.

"Mind if I join? Just to, uh..." *Make sure no one else sees, especially not Kirk.*

"Sure." Mac left the room.

Katherine followed him out and down the staircase. She didn't want to fill the air with awkward chitchat, but also didn't want to leave an even more awkward silence hanging over them the entire way down to the gate. Reaching the front doors, she started in with, "I've got this puzzle and I think if I sketch it up, I might figure it out."

"Puzzle?" His eyes lit up.

She opened the left door and held it for him. "Yeah."

He passed through. "What kind?"

She followed him down the hill. "Good question. Not sure I know."

"Logic? Riddle? Anagram? Pattern-matching?"

"Didn't even know there were so many. Probably logographic. It involves symbols."

# THE FALL OF BLACKSTONE MANSION

"That you're gonna draw?"

"Yeah."

"This isn't a puzzle you're designing?"

"No."

"So you're drawing it from memory?"

"Yeah."

His brow furrowed with intense intrigue. "Huh."

They reached the gate. This time, he opened the right door and held it for her.

"Thank you, sir," she said.

"No problem, boss." He pointed to a nearby orange truck. "Over here." He unlocked the passenger side, opened the glove compartment, and took out a notepad and pen. He presented the items to her like a college president handing over a degree. "Ma'am."

"Thanks." She accepted them. "Can I...?" She pointed to the side of the truck.

"By all means."

She leaned against the truck and started a very rough sketch, an outline of a playing-card diamond.

"That one of the symbols?" he asked.

"Not quite." She drew the entryway hall's symbol—the one missing the V—right below the diamond's bottom point and continued clockwise until she'd matched each tower's symbol to each of the diamond's points.

"Wait. That's the mansion."

"Yep."

"So, what's the puzzle you're trying to solve?"

"Remember how in the entryway hall Kirk had to push that metal symbol into the wall, then down?"

"I remember that door opening on the side of the staircase."

"Right. Well, in order to do that, he had to do the thing with the symbol."

"All right."

She tapped the pen in the center of the diamond. "There's another place here, deep inside the building, where there's another symbol." She quickly drew the pendant's symbol where she'd tapped the pen.

"Another doorway?"

"Yes..." She dragged out the word because technically, it wasn't a doorway, but he was effectively right.

"How's it open?"

She looked up at him. "That's the puzzle."

"I see." His tone suggested that ideas were flooding his mind. "Mind if I...?" He opened his palm to accept the pen.

"Not at all." She placed it in his hand.

"Kirk had to push down on this one." He tapped the symbol at the diamond's bottom point.

"Yeah."

Mac drew a little arrow pointing down from the bottom symbol. "I'm guessing to open each other doorway, you had to do the same with the other symbols." He drew little arrows pointing away from each of the diamond's respective points.

"That's right."

"What if you did the opposite for the middle one?"

"You mean...?"

"If the way you opened all the other doorways was pushing those symbols"—he tapped each of the diamond's points—"away from the middle, what if the way you open the middle is by pushing them toward it?"

"Together."

"Right."

"To match the middle symbol!"

"Yeah!"

"Oh my God, Mac, you're a genius!"

He laughed. "Nah, I just play an epic ass-ton of video games."

"But wait. How am I gonna be able to push each of those symbols toward the center one?"

"Unless your arms grow a lot longer..."

"But... Come on. Let's get back." She handed him the pen. She then tore off the page, folded it up, and stuffed it in her pocket.

"Yes, ma'am."

They hurried up the hill so fast, she had to pause at the carriage loop to take a few breaths. They then ran up to the boudoir.

## AUGUSTINE PIERCE

Kirk and Shane were finishing wrapping up a sofa when Katherine and Mac burst in.

"Change of plans!" she announced.

## 19

"Are you sure you wanna do this?" Kirk asked.

"It'll solve everything! Everything I've been trying to figure out since I first set foot in this house!" Katherine explained.

They were standing near the mansion's front doors, trying to keep their voices down in front of the rest of the crew, who'd gathered at the bottom of the staircase awaiting further instructions.

"I really don't think it's a good idea," Kirk said.

"Maybe it isn't, but, Kirk, I have to know."

"You gonna tell Jordan?"

"Tell him what?" She threw the rest of the guys a nervous glance, hoping they didn't catch on to the fact that Kirk was referring to everyone's boss.

"About whatever we find down there."

"I don't know what we're gonna find down there."

"You never followed up, did you?"

"On what?"

He spoke at a normal volume. "On the fact that those tombs all had dead Blackstones in them!"

She smiled at the crew to assure them that yes, everything was okay.

"They still do!" Kirk exclaimed.

She seized his arm, marched him outside, and closed the door behind them. "Would you *please* keep your voice down?"

"Kat, what the hell?"

"I did follow up, but..."

"But what?"

She explained the entire complicated situation. The more detail she gave, the more Kirk calmed.

Finally, he sighed and shook his head. "That is the weirdest thing I've ever heard in my entire frickin' life!"

"Look, we've found everyone Marcus murdered. Whatever's down there is probably just some other dusty old library."

"Which you're not gonna tell Jordan about."

"I dunno. Yes. Maybe. Eventually, okay?"

"If he gets pissed 'cause you didn't tell him and drops these recording sessions he's setting up for me..."

"He wouldn't punish you for something I did."

Kirk's eyebrows raised with intense skepticism.

*Okay, yeah, he probably would.* "Whatever happens, I swear I'll take full responsibility, but right now, I need everyone's help."

# THE FALL OF BLACKSTONE MANSION

Kirk opened the door, held it for her, and nodded to the crew.

"We ready to go?" Shane asked.

"Yep," Kirk confirmed.

"What's the plan?" Mac asked.

"I'm gonna post one of you in each of the mansion's towers," Katherine explained. "Since cell coverage is crap, we'll coordinate with these." She held up her walkie-talkie. "When I say go, each of the four's gonna activate their symbol."

Ross raised his hand.

"I'll show you where, how, all that stuff," she assured.

Ross lowered his hand.

"Kirk, since you handled this tower last time..." She pointed to the symbol at the top of the staircase.

Kirk nodded, but bit his lip, as if to stop himself from declaring what a terrible idea he thought this all was. He took out his flashlight, clicked it on, and marched up the staircase.

Katherine and the others also turned on their flashlights and followed him. "Go ahead and activate this one," she said.

Kirk pressed the symbol into the wall. The sounds of wood *scraping* against wood echoed within. He looked back at her.

"Now up," she said.

Kirk slid the symbol. Wood *scraped* and metal *clicked*. After moving it about an inch and a half, he stopped. "Looks like that's it."

"Nothing happened," Ross said.

"Yet." Katherine nodded at Kirk. "Let go."

Kirk released the symbol and faced the others.

She turned on her walkie-talkie. "Kirk's gonna stay here. Everybody else, let's go to the next one."

The group continued on to the west tower, where she placed Shane at the symbol. "To the right," she instructed.

Shane activated the symbol. *Grind!* Stone slid against stone.

"Great," she declared. "Shane stays here. Everyone else..." She beckoned them to follow.

They soon reached the north tower.

"Ross, you're here," she said.

"Okay. Push down?"

"You got it. When I give the signal."

She and the rest of the crew then moved to the east tower. She presented the symbol as if it were some kind of lifetime achievement award. "Mac, since you figured it out..."

"Don't mind if I do." He walked right up to the symbol. He pressed it in and to the left. *Grind!*

"Everybody else, follow me." She led the remaining group to Silas's bust in the west-east hallway,

# THE FALL OF BLACKSTONE MANSION

then called over the walkie-talkie. "All right, guys. Wait for my signal, then punch it."

"Roger. Over," Kirk said.

"Ditto. Over," Shane said.

"Same. Over," Mac said.

"You got it," Ross said. "And over."

"Let's do this." Katherine turned to the bust. She went through the steps to reveal the corkscrew staircase.

As the wall revolved to expose it, the guys all reacted with a series of "Ooh," "Ahh," and "Whoa."

"What is *up* with this place?" Randy asked.

"Off we go, gentlemen." Katherine descended the staircase, passed through the tunnel, and parked before the central tower. She clicked off her flashlight and put it back in her purse.

Dennis got a closer look at the tower's affixed symbol. "So weird."

She eased him back with a gentle push. "Easy there."

Wandering around the tower, Randy gazed up at the ceiling's glass plates and metal beams. "Damn. That's a pretty good sized lightning rod. Thick-ass wire too."

Katherine followed him. "What are you...?" She glanced up. A giant lightning rod stood directly over the center of the tower. From it, the same wire she'd seen the electricians and other workmen installing beneath the scaffolding snaked across the ceiling. "Let's, uh, stay focused."

She led him back to the rest of the group and pointed to the seams in the floor that outlined another set of descending steps.

"Oh, gotcha," Dennis said.

She called on her walkie-talkie. "You guys ready?"

Kirk, Shane, and Mac all responded in the affirmative.

"So it's down, right?" Ross asked.

"That's right," Katherine confirmed. "Punch it."

Nothing happened.

She looked down at the floor's seams. Nothing had moved or shifted. She called on her walkie-talkie. "Guys?"

No one answered.

She walked several steps away from the group and called again. "Kirk? You there?"

"Affirmative. Over," Kirk answered.

"What happened?"

"No idea. I pressed the symbol, was trying to slide it up, when I felt this intense cold wash over my hand like I'd stuck it in ice water. Felt like the other night when we—"

"Yeah." She cut him off, not wanting him to fill in the blanks of the other times they'd been here poking around. *Vernon. What does he want now?* "Shane? Ross? Mac? You guys okay?"

"Yeah, somethin' similar, but I'm good. Over," Shane said.

"Same here. Over," Ross said.

"All good. Over," Mac said.

*If he's coming after us, we'd better get to it.* "Punch it." She joined the others in front of the tower.

*Griiind!* Stone against metal. The sound was intense. The ground vibrated. The steps outlined within the seams in the floor did as she'd predicted. One lowered a few inches. The next sank to twice the depth. The process continued counterclockwise all the way around the tower, forming a new spiral staircase. Its last step's descent also revealed both a lever built into the wall on the tower side and the opening of a tunnel that disappeared under the first step.

Katherine nodded, admiring it all. "Beautiful." She called on her walkie-talkie. "Kirk?"

"Yeah?"

"You guys can come down."

"Roger. Over and out."

"Careful on your way down," she told the group behind her as she set her foot on the first step.

The entire area vibrated with a low, rumbling *groan* that exploded out of the tunnel behind them, rocketed past them, and dissipated in a trembling echo beyond. The group looked all around for the source.

"What the hell was *that*?" Dennis asked.

*Definitely Vernon.* "Nothing. Let's go." She hurried down the next few steps.

"Didn't sound like nothing."

Katherine waved for the group to follow. "Let's just... Come on—"

A shadow flew out from the tunnel and raced across the floor, straight for them.

Straight for her.

A few of the guys looked up, likely expecting a bird or some other obstruction in the ceiling's light that was casting the solid black, blurry humanoid shape.

The sky was clear.

Katherine dove out of the shadow's path and hit the ground with a pained grunt. Dennis and Randy helped her to her feet. "Thanks."

She didn't have a moment to say anything else as the shadow launched up the side of the tower to its symbol, where it lingered, twisting and roiling. As she'd seen with previous spirits, two sets of five white spots began to push through the surface of the river rocks like festering wounds about to burst.

"What is goin' on, boss?" Randy asked.

Katherine didn't answer. Instead, she watched the shadow like the rest of them, wondering what it was going to do next.

She didn't have to wonder for long as, out of the left of her periphery, shot a second shadow down the wall, across the floor, and up the tower, where it blasted the first away from the symbol.

"What was *that*?" Dennis asked.

*Good question. Looked like one spirit fighting off another.*

"What'd we miss?" Kirk asked.

Katherine turned around to see him arrive with Shane, Ross, and Mac. "Nothing. Just a—"

Dennis stepped forward. "Nothing? What're you *talking* about?"

"Hey, man, watch the tone," Kirk warned.

Dennis didn't even look at him. "I dunno what I just saw, but whatever it was, it wasn't frickin'... natural."

Katherine stood between the tower and the crew. "All right, listen up. The lightest of you outweighs me by double, but if a trick of the light bothers you that much, front door's that way." She pointed. "I wanna know what the hell is buried beneath this mansion. You're either with me or you're on your way home. Doesn't matter to me."

Shane quietly grumbled, "Leave now and we won't get paid."

Dennis pointed to the tower. "Screw that, screw this, and screw you guys." He marched out.

"Anybody else?" Katherine asked.

The rest of the crew murmured and glanced at each other.

Mac smiled with excitement. "With ya, boss!"

She nodded at him, then started down the steps. Kirk followed right behind. The rest filed in after. Entering the tunnel under the first step, she took out and turned on her flashlight. The beam cast long shadows down the stairs before it dropped off into cold black.

"How far's this go?" Randy asked.

"I don't know," Katherine said.

Seconds passed. Finally, the floor leveled out. While she wasn't sure how long the descent lasted, it seemed like it was about the same amount of time as the ones she'd made into the tombs. That meant that they were likely not much farther underground than she'd been in them.

She shone her light all around the vast, chilly space. The beam danced across a gallery of stone columns that thrust up from the floor and curved into the ceiling at pointed Gothic arches. There were so many spread out so far, it was difficult to tell how deep the area stretched. She guessed, though, that it was likely as big as the floor above.

"Where the hell are we?" Shane asked.

"Some kind of basement?" Randy asked.

"More like crypt," Mac observed.

*Good word for it, Mac.* "I'm looking around."

"Careful," Kirk warned.

## THE FALL OF BLACKSTONE MANSION

"I know," Katherine assured him. *They didn't build a giant, empty space. Must be something here.*

She wandered among the columns, neither sure of what she was looking for nor how to find it. It wasn't lost on her that without their flashlights, it would have been impossible to navigate these columns in the dark.

A sparkle. She aimed her light back where she thought she saw it. Refracted beams danced in gleaming glass. She stopped, looked up, and shone her light in a slow, horizontal arc.

From the top of the column on her left, a metal arm reached down toward the column on her right. Nearly halfway between, the arm met a frame shaped exactly like the pendant, though slightly bigger. Within the frame lay a thick glass lens. The frame-and-lens apparatus hung only a few inches above her sight line. A second arm connected the apparatus to the right column.

*That's something.* She took a step toward the apparatus. On closer inspection, its frame wasn't exactly the same shape as the pendant, rather its outline. There was the equilateral triangle on top, a V on the bottom, but no connecting lines between.

A silver band, like those embedded in the tombs' floors, was attached to the top of the apparatus's lens and extended to the ceiling.

She reached up to the apparatus to feel for any further physical traits—grooves or notches—that might better show its relationship to the pendant, how the latter might fit into the former.

Black lines scrawled across dark gray stone. Through the lens, and with the aid of her flashlight, she realized she was staring at a wall a few yards away. Someone had drawn the pendant's symbol on its surface, six feet in diameter. *No, not drawn. Burned!*

"Kat?" Kirk's voice sounded both curious and wary.

"Coming!" She turned around to find the group standing only a few feet away from the opposite side of the tower from where they'd all descended.

She walked over and eased past them. There stood a huge metal door built into the tower's wall. It had a porthole near its top and a door-locking wheel—the same as those found on submarine hatches—halfway up its left side.

She laid her fingers on the wheel.

"A lot more intense than a brass knob," Kirk observed.

"Yeah," Katherine said.

"You sure you wanna open that thing?" Ross asked.

Katherine didn't answer. She wrapped her fingers around the wheel and attempted a rotation.

It didn't budge.

# THE FALL OF BLACKSTONE MANSION

"Maybe one of you big, strong boys?" She stepped aside.

Kirk gripped the wheel and gave it a good twist to the right. Grunting, he kept going.

"You sure you got that?" Shane grinned.

"Shut up." Kirk gave the wheel the last three turns.

Like that of an ancient church bell, a low tone rang out as the door opened a crack.

Kirk stepped back and nodded at Katherine. "All yours."

She eased the door open all the way and stepped inside. A faint light trickled down from above. Looking up, she saw a distant, bright circle of sky light. *The top of the tower. It's open.* At the center of the circle, she recognized the bottom of the lightning rod Randy had pointed out. The wire was connected to one side of the rod. A silver band was connected to the other side, from which it crossed to the brim of the tower, where it ran down its wall. She followed the band all the way to several inches above her head, where it split in two. One half branched off at a ninety-degree angle to the right, toward somewhere above the door. *It go to that lens thing?* The other half continued down to directly in front of her.

At the height of the band's division, there hung suspended a fine, silver mirror, the size of the porthole. Four bars drilled into the tower's wall held it in place, aimed at the door at a forty-five-degree angle. It cast a harsh shadow over everything below it.

She shone her flashlight straight ahead, where she discovered the lidless top of a concrete coffin identical to the other ones she'd found. Beyond it, her beam caught the metallic glint of the band where it ended behind the head of the coffin.

She continued toward the coffin. As she neared it, her light caught a band embedded in the floor, which ran from the coffin to under the door. A quick sweep of the floor located two more bands, each one running from the coffin's sides to those of the tower. *This is where the circuit connectors go! From all the other coffins! But what are they doing here?*

She reached the coffin, but waited till the others joined her before she shone her light on what lay inside.

The beam fell on the unmistakable, and though so very long dead, perfectly preserved face of none other than the mansion's builder and dynasty's founder, Silas Blackstone.

## 20

"Nope!" Shane declared to Silas's corpse, which was dressed in the finest three-piece suit money could have bought in his time. Shane then gave an about-face and marched out of the tomb.

"Where you going?" Katherine demanded.

Shane turned around. "Dead guys buried in weird-ass underground bank vault chambers opened with even weirder occult symbols is where I draw the line!" He resumed his exit. "Should've drawn the line at skeleton chicks buried under the floor."

"There's so much more we have to...!" Katherine called after him.

"Have a blast, Kat! I'm out!" Shane's voice faded as he disappeared up the stairs.

Katherine surveyed the rest of their faces. She saw some fear, some intrigue, but mostly men who were waiting for her word on what to do next.

"I dunno," Mac spoke up. "I think it's all kinda cool."

"Maybe we should be heading out," Kirk advised.

"But, Kirk..." Katherine started. *There's so much more! I'm so close! I can feel it!*

"We can always come back."

Katherine nodded. "You're right. We should go." She turned to leave. "Can always come back." She wasn't sure about that. There was already so much tension between her and Jordan and he was probably looking into her activity in the private study, so if she had a window within which to return and continue any investigation, it was likely closing quickly.

As she exited the tomb, she faced the others. "Can we, uh...?" She rotated her finger in the air to indicate sealing the door behind them.

"We got it." Kirk waited while the other guys left, then closed the door and sealed it tight.

As Katherine headed back up the steps, she thought out loud. "Maybe tomorrow, maybe next week." *Another week's too late. If I'm gonna get to the bottom of this mansion, so to speak, gotta do it now.*

At the back of the line, Ross called up. "I don't know about you guys, but I need a drink."

# THE FALL OF BLACKSTONE MANSION

Katherine took the tiniest sip from her chocolate stout and stared past the bar at her reflection in the beer-brand mirror. She and the guys had come to Sean's Irish Pub and Grill near Blackstone's town square. She hadn't been here since the night she'd first seen Eileen's ghost. That horrific sight had so traumatized her that she'd slammed one shot after another until she'd practically tumbled off her stool and Kirk had to take her home.

"Usually a bit more effective if you drink the whole thing." Kirk stood next to her.

She looked at him, but was so distracted, she barely spoke. "Huh?"

"Your beer. You can drink it. I'm driving."

Her eyes found her pint. She regarded it as if she'd never seen beer before. "Not thirsty."

"Guys asked me to thank you again for the beers."

"Uh-huh."

He nodded and smiled, then seeming to understand that she needed a moment, he retreated to his crew.

She watched them in the mirror, with their convivial chatting and joking, that to her distracted mind sounded like nothing but distant mumbling. She was envious of their ability to wash down everything they'd seen today. She had the fleeting desire to join in, but decided against it. She was far too focused on putting together the latest pieces they'd found of the mansion's puzzle.

*Five silver bands. Four going in to Silas's coffin. One coming out. Off to that lens thing.* She eased her beer aside and set her purse on the bar. She unzipped it and slid out the pendant, hardly concerned with who saw it or what they'd think.

She murmured to herself as she pressed a finger to each of the pendant's four points. "We found Eileen in the west tower, Gloria in the south, Reginald in the east, Vernon in the north. Now Silas in the center." She double tapped the purse's cloth under the middle of the pendant. "Marcus murdered Gloria, Reginald, and Vernon, but couldn't have murdered Silas 'cause he died decades before Marcus was born. So that's not the connection."

Katherine traced four invisible lines from the pendant's four corners to its center. "The four silver connectors were going to Silas from the other family members. And Eileen. The family members, Eileen, to Silas."

Katherine thought back to the vision Eileen's ghost had given her of Eileen's initial burial in Silas's grave in the family cemetery. Then to Eileen's final words to Vernon. *It's yours.* She lifted her eyes to the mirror. *Eileen wasn't a blood relative...* She informed her reflection, "But her unborn baby was!"

# THE FALL OF BLACKSTONE MANSION

The floodgates had opened. The puzzle pieces smashed together. *Miles's friend Nigel said the pendant's symbol was ancient. Occult. Representing a door or a key to the cosmos.* "Or another realm." *Marcus mentioned the Formula and the Realm to Reginald, that he'd found reference to them in Silas's notes.* "Notes that disappeared from the hidden study." *Marcus then wore the pendant around his neck when he sealed Vernon in his tomb.* "Marcus must've found the notes *after* he'd murdered Eileen and buried her in Silas's grave! He needed all blood relatives—the Formula—so he dug her back up and reburied her in the west tower! That's why we found her there!"

Katherine stood up and away from the bar. "But then we buried her in a real cemetery. She couldn't be exhumed without a court order. Which leaves her tomb empty. Has to be a blood relative." Her jaw dropped open with the realization. "C!"

"Kirky give you that for your month-iversary?" Ross asked with very slurred speech. "Pretty weird-lookin' necklace." He reached for the pendant.

She pressed her left hand over it and commanded him, "Don't touch it!" She instinctively pushed him away.

He flew across the room, smashing into the wall.

All chatter, all beer sipping, all pool playing, all activity ceased.

"Kat?" Kirk asked.

It took her a second to locate him among the many faces staring at her. He stood about four feet away with his palms up in surrender, inching toward her. She threw a glance at Ross. He looked far more shocked at what had just happened than physically injured.

"You okay?" Kirk was now almost in her personal space.

Ross grumbled. "Is *she* okay?"

She kept her eyes on Ross. "I'm sorry. I didn't mean..." She knew her intention hardly mattered. She'd planted him into the wall without so much as a flick of her wrist. That's all everyone saw.

"I know." Kirk now stood right next to her. "Why don't we...?" He pointed to the door.

"Yeah." She was not in a position to disagree. She was, in fact, lucky if Ross didn't press charges.

Collecting the pendant and her purse, she did her best to put the former back into the latter as she made her way to the door. She kept her head dipped so as not to make eye contact with anyone.

Once outside, she waited about a minute for Kirk to arrive. She was ready to offer any number of excuses, but his soothing voice beat her to it. "Let's get you home."

"What about their drinks? Getting home?" This night was feeling like the one only weeks ago when

# THE FALL OF BLACKSTONE MANSION

she'd first encountered Eileen's ghost. Kirk had to take care of her then too.

"Don't worry about that." He walked her to his truck's passenger side and opened the door.

She put on her seat belt as he closed the door. Before he'd reached the driver's side, she shoved the pendant the rest of the way into her purse. She didn't even want him to see the black-and-platinum piece for fear that he'd badger her about her obsession with it. *He'd be right, though. I am obsessed.*

He closed his door and fired up the engine. He said nothing for a long time.

She listened to the tires on the road and kept her eyes fixed on the horizon.

He inhaled sharply, clearly ready to dive straight into it. "You barely touched him, Kat."

She only nodded because she didn't know what to say.

"I mean, barely," he said. "And he flew like you shot him out a cannon."

"I didn't wanna—"

"It's that thing, isn't it?" He peered down at her lap.

*So much for keeping his attention away from it.* "I don't know."

"I think you do. At first, it was just you were, like, stroking it and stuff. Now you're hurting people."

"I didn't mean to—"

"You should get rid of it."

"No!" She sounded far more insistent than she'd intended.

He sighed. "Kat, either you get rid of it or I will."

"I can't!"

"Why not?"

"Because it's the key!"

"To what?"

"All of it!" She finally had the courage to look at him. "Everything. From Eileen's death to Silas's body."

"What?"

"The body we found today. It's the guy who built the mansion. He engineered the whole thing. The tombs, the structure of the house, that weird-ass lens thing that's the same shape as the pendant thing." She patted her purse to indicate its contents. "It's at the center of all of it and I need to keep it safe with me, because even with everything that's gone down at the mansion, it's not over."

"What are you talking about?"

"C."

"What?"

"No, who. Jordan's cousin Stacey."

"What about her?"

"I think he may be planning to use her somehow. In some kind of ritual or something."

"Kat..."

## THE FALL OF BLACKSTONE MANSION

"I need to warn her. Before it's too late. Jordan mentioned the eighteenth. He ordered the PGE crew to be done by then. What's so significant about that date?"

"Not Thanksgiving."

"No, it's gotta be something else." She took out her phone, opened a web browser, and searched November eighteenth. She read the results out loud. "National Camp Day, World Toilet Day, National Have a Bad Day Day." She gasped. "Oh my God."

"What?"

"The full moon."

"So?"

"So he's probably gonna kill her in some weird, full moon blood ritual!"

"Kat, come on."

They pulled up to his place. She ignored him and rang Stacey. He sat patiently as she waited for Stacey to answer.

"Hello?" Stacey sounded like she didn't recognize the number.

"Hey, C, it's Kat."

"Oh, hey. What's up?"

"Are you at home?"

"Yeah. Why?"

"Alone?"

"Yeah. What's goin' on?"

"What's your address?"

Stacey hesitantly gave it to her.

"Hold tight," Katherine said. "Don't go anywhere. I'll be there in less than an hour."

"Um, okay. What's this about?"

"Too much to explain over the phone. See you soon." She hung up and gave Kirk pleading eyes. "You don't have to come, but I gotta go."

"No, of course I'll come. Might wanna take your car, though. Better gas mileage."

They got out of his truck and into her car. They were quiet most of the forty minutes to Stacey's neighborhood in east Portland. Arriving at her street, they found a boxy, gray, rundown apartment complex. Next to Katherine's, it looked about two steps away from homelessness.

"This it?" Kirk asked.

"Think so." Katherine double checked the address. "Yep." She parked and ran up to the complex's entrance.

He trailed her, most likely trying to stay out of the way.

She called Stacey's unit and texted her.

> Here.

The door *buzzed* open, and she ran to Stacey's floor. There she waited for what seemed like ten minutes before Stacey opened it.

# THE FALL OF BLACKSTONE MANSION

"Hey, so, what's...?" Stacey asked as Kirk arrived. "Kirk, right?"

He smiled. "Like the captain."

"You sure you're alone?" Katherine asked.

"Yeah," Stacey said.

"Can we come in?"

"Um, you're kinda freakin' me out." Stacey stepped out of her apartment and closed the door behind her.

*Guess we're gonna do this here.* "C, one of my jobs for Jordan has been selling off his estate. The antiques."

Stacey nodded. "I remember."

"Well, part of that job is to comb through all his stuff to find those pieces."

"Uh-huh."

"Over the last several days, weeks, I've found some really weird stuff." Katherine took the pendant out of her purse and held it up by its silver chain.

"What is *that*?" Stacey reached for it.

*Don't touch it!* Katherine's mind screamed at her, but she held back that instinct.

Stacey gripped the piece. "Heavy."

"This thing, this pendant, not only can no one identify the metal, but its shape, the symbol?"

Stacey nodded.

"Some kind of ancient, occult whatever." Katherine filled in the blanks of everything she'd experienced. The mansion's towers' symbol-switches, their tombs, the bodies they contained, right up to what she and Kirk's crew had discovered today. She left out the ghosts and their visions.

"That's... incredible," Stacey said.

"Look, I know Jordan's kinda taken you under his wing, but the next time he reaches out, ignore him. In fact, if you can, get outta town for a few days. At least till the eighteenth."

"Why?"

"It's for your own good. Trust me."

"Yeah. I'll, uh, think about that."

*Did I not get through to her?* "C, ignore him, get outta town."

"Yeah. Yeah. Of course. Yeah." Stacey nodded emphatically. She placed her hand on her doorknob. "I'm gonna..."

"All right." Katherine backed away. "Have a good night, C."

"You too." Stacey nodded at them both, then went inside, and closed the door.

Katherine faced Kirk. "Let's go home."

"So we're not showing up at all?" Randy asked Katherine over the phone.

# THE FALL OF BLACKSTONE MANSION

She and Kirk were on their way back to Creek. She'd given the crew a break on Sunday, even though that meant leaving the work unfinished.

"That's right," she said. "Day off."

"But we were right in the middle of—"

"It's okay. Don't worry about it. Kirk or I'll reach out when we pick it up again."

"Okay, Kat. Thanks for letting me know."

"One more thing?"

"Yeah?"

"Remember that lightning rod you noticed on top of the tower?"

"How could I forget it? Biggest one I've ever seen."

"You know much about electricity?"

"Licensed and bonded, so only a little."

She grinned. "What would such a thing be used for?"

"Normally, to disperse the flow away from a house, into the ground."

"But in this case?"

"Whoever put it there might've wanted to power something. Something huge."

*The silver connectors. To the concrete coffins. To that lens. But why? No machinery.* "What if someone turned on the power connected to that wire?"

"I dunno why they would. They'd likely knock out the whole county."

"That kinda power, how well would it conduct through those silver bands?"

"Better than anything else."

She inhaled sharply. *Jordan's gonna electrocute C!* She forced a calm voice. "Thanks, Randy."

"Any time." He hung up.

Katherine planted her phone in her lap.

"That the last of 'em?" Kirk asked.

She nodded.

"All right," he said.

"Jordan's gonna murder Stacey, Kirk."

"You warned her. That's all you can do."

"I hope."

They were silent the remaining twenty minutes to his apartment. Once settled in, they went to bed and he passed out. She couldn't sleep. Not for a long time. *I warned her. That's all I can do.*

To distract herself into sleep, she picked her phone up from the nightstand, plugged in her earbuds, and got down to a lengthy game of *Fruit Ninja*.

## 21

The next day was a lazy one. Katherine and Kirk woke up late, then tried the breakfast place he'd suggested during their spat the previous Saturday.

The food was excellent. So much so that other than ordering their meals, they said very little as they ate.

She was still thinking about their Saturday mansion discoveries, putting things together at Sean's, and her attempt at warning Stacey. *She probably didn't even care. Probably went to bed and forgot all about the fact that we dropped by.*

She eyed Kirk. She'd been feeling a distance growing between them since she'd admitted she hadn't told him about seeing the man in black when they were out with Jordan and Fae. It had only gotten worse, and she wasn't sure how to bridge the gap. She knew he still cared about her, knew he wasn't looking for a way out, but beyond that, she didn't know what to do. She hoped that their impending move to California might change all that, but she suspected that the chasm between them was only deepening.

"What you lookin' at?" he asked.

"You." She smiled.

He smiled back, but said nothing else.

Soon, they finished and headed home. The rest of the evening was brief, as he wanted to be up early Monday morning to catch up on some work he'd neglected on Friday.

---

Katherine stood before Kirk's dining table, her eyes stuck on the pendant lying flat in the middle. As much as she burned to touch it, she was holding off. She knew that if she did, she'd sit here all day doing nothing else. But she also lacked the strength to ignore the piece for very long.

She took out her phone and called El Toro, the restaurant she was supposed to meet with today.

"You guys canceled the appointment," the owner said.

"What do you mean we… Who did you speak with?"

"Johnny or Jack or something."

"Jordan?"

# THE FALL OF BLACKSTONE MANSION

"That's right. Yeah, he was real apologetic. Said he'd already found someone. I told him no big deal. Happens all the time."

"Right." *I knew it! Canceled La Muse, now El Toro. Maybe he did have Fae make catering arrangements. Or he wanted to clear his schedule for his weird-ass full moon bloodfest.*

*Fae.* She'd already warned Stacey, but as much as she hated to admit it, she knew she also needed to warn Fae. While she most likely had no role to play in Jordan's plans for the mansion, Katherine suspected anyone who had any close association with him was in for real trouble.

"I should call her," she told the pendant. "No, I should drive up." The second she said it out loud, she knew it was true. Were she to call Fae, all the other woman had to do was ignore her. If she drove to Fae's office, though, at least she could make a memorable scene that might convince Fae to at least consider her warning.

Katherine scooped up the pendant, put it in her purse, and headed out. The drive to Fae's part of Portland was about an hour away, so she had plenty of time to consider how she'd handle their encounter.

"'Fae, your boyfriend's crazy.' No, too simple and childish. 'Fae, we need to talk about Jordan.' No, that opens you up to, 'Why do *we* need to talk about him?'"

She couldn't think of anything better before she arrived in the city's southeast trendy industrial quarter. She soon located F+E Events' headquarters, housed in a former warehouse. Parking on a side street, she marched up to the front door with all the determination in the world, but still no idea how to tackle the conversation she was about to have.

Approaching the receptionist, a young woman seated behind an ultra-slick desk of polished steel and glass, Katherine went for unbridled confidence. "I need to speak to Fae."

"And you are?" the receptionist asked.

"Katherine Norrington."

The receptionist regarded her as if she'd crawled in from straight out of the sewer. "Did you have an appointment?"

"She'll wanna see me."

The receptionist hesitated, likely calculating the trouble she'd get in if she didn't summon Fae versus if she did. "One second. Stay right there."

Katherine nodded. The receptionist ran off to a metal staircase leading up to another level. She knocked on, then entered a glass-walled office. Katherine overheard a timid whisper.

"What the hell is *she* doing here?" Fae asked with severe incredulity.

## THE FALL OF BLACKSTONE MANSION

Katherine heard more timid whispers, then staccato footsteps stamping the metal floor. Fae emerged the next second with her receptionist in tow. The two women descended the stairs.

Fae marched right up to Katherine. "What the hell do you want?"

"Fae, look, I know we're not the best of friends," Katherine began.

Fae dipped her head to give Katherine her signature intense eye roll.

"It's about Jordan," Katherine continued.

Fae waved it off. "Oh, you can have him."

"What?"

"Yeah, I'm done with him. And all his white male entitlement and privilege."

*None of which seemed to bother you before.* "Gotcha. So you're not seeing him?"

"What did you think I meant by 'done with him'?"

The receptionist grinned.

"Okay, well, since you're not seeing him," Katherine said, "I guess there's no need to warn you."

"Warn me? About what?" Fae asked.

*How could I explain it all here? Now?* "Nothing. Never mind. Doesn't matter."

"Yep. His big ol' pile of inheritance is all yours for the plucking."

"I was never interested in Jordan or his money."

"Whatevs. Don't care. Have a grand day." Fae spun on her heel and headed back up to her office.

The receptionist watched her until she started back up the stairs, then faced Katherine. "Did you need your parking validated?"

---

Katherine was almost back at Kirk's place when she decided to drive to his work. Due to the distance she'd been feeling between them, she thought that her showing up and maybe taking him to dinner would be a delightful surprise.

Pulling into the parking lot, she spotted something that completely threw her.

Kirk's truck was missing.

*Maybe he's out running an errand.* She parked and headed for the building's entrance, when she remembered her last exchange with Annie, Kirk's coworker. Katherine had accused Annie of being in love with Kirk and when Annie had denied it, Katherine had doubled down. *Awkward.* It wasn't the nicest thing to have done, but she justified it because Annie hadn't been nice to her either.

Sucking up her pride, Katherine opened the door. "Kirk here?"

Annie looked up from her computer, paused a second, likely wondering why Katherine had graced the office with her presence, then answered with a curt, frustrated-sounding, "Nope."

"He out?"

"Nope."

"So where is he?"

"You tell me."

"How would I know?"

"Aren't you two *living* together?" Annie's voice boiled with jealousy.

*Guess I was right about her having the hots for him.* "Yeah, but I don't track his every step."

"Well, he never showed."

"What?"

"Never showed. I've been on my own all day."

"That doesn't make any sense. Did he call?"

"Nope. And I've tried him a bunch of times."

"That's crazy." Katherine took out her phone.

"No kidding. He's never done anything like this. I mean, I hate the job too, but I'd at least have warned him before quitting."

Katherine called Kirk. "He wasn't gonna quit yet."

"Yet?"

*Crap. Cat outta the bag.* "I'm trying him now."

Kirk's phone rang and rang, then went to voice mail.

"Weird," Katherine said. "Usually he picks up."

"Well, he hasn't all day."

"You've been calling him all day?"

Annie sounded very defensive, as if Katherine were accusing her of coming after her man. "Yeah, 'cause he never showed."

"Thanks, Annie." Katherine left.

She floored it to Kirk's apartment and practically smashed the door off its hinges as she burst in. "Baby? Kirk?"

No one answered.

She didn't bother to close the door as she ran into the bedroom.

He wasn't there.

She stormed into the bathroom and tore open the shower.

No Kirk.

She retreated into the living area. "Oh my God, oh my God..." She took out her phone and made quick calls to each of his crew but Ross. None of them had heard from him.

Anticipating friction over her and Ross's incident at the bar, she led with a rushed apology. "Listen, Ross, I am so sorry—"

"Kat, you were drunk. I got in your space. Nothin' else needs to be said."

*Actually, I was stone sober.* "I appreciate that. Have you heard from Kirk? I haven't been able to reach him."

"No. Everything okay?"

# THE FALL OF BLACKSTONE MANSION

"I'm sure it's fine. Thanks." She hung up and shoved her phone back into her pocket. "Not here. Not at work. Hasn't answered his phone for Annie or me." She cupped her hands over her mouth and breathed into her palms. "Gotta just…"

Not knowing what else to do, she sat on the couch. She took out her phone and called Kirk. His line rang and rang until it went to voice mail. She hung up and repeated this process. Over and over again.

She shoved her phone back in her pocket and asked out loud, "How long before I can report a missing person?" She leapt to her feet, retrieved her laptop, sat back down with it, and searched. "I can do it now?" She hesitated before taking out her phone again. "If I file a report and he just shows up, I'll look like the crazy girlfriend to the police. Not to mention Kirk."

Considering their strained relationship, she waited. She logged on to a streaming service and picked the longest, most boring documentary series she could find. She got comfortable on the couch as she settled in for the long haul.

*Buzz!* Her phone vibrating against her leg woke her up.

"Oh, thank God!" She took the device out of her pocket and checked the ID. It was Jordan. "What the hell are you…?" she asked the screen, then answered, "Hey, Jordan, kind of in the middle of something."

"Kat?" His voice was thick, as if he were worried, on the verge of tears, or otherwise deeply troubled.

*Unless you know where he is.* "Has Kirk said anything to you? You guys chatting your label or something?"

Jordan took a deep breath. "Katherine? Kirk is fine."

"Oh great! So you guys did meet up! Where are you? And why hasn't he answered his phone? Why didn't he show up for work?"

Jordan paused for a good long time. "Katherine, I'm going to need you to come out to the mansion."

"Mansion? Why would I do that? Where's Kirk, Jordan?"

"Kirk is fine, but he won't be if you don't come out to the mansion and bring the necklace thing you've been hiding."

Katherine walked over to the couch and sat. "Jordan, what the hell are you talking about?"

"Please, Katherine, let's not make this any harder than it needs to be. Come to the mansion. Bring the necklace. Kirk will be fine." He paused and she could hear a voice in the background. "No police," he continued. "No contact with anyone else. Come now."

"Jordan, what the hell have you done?"

He paused again. This time so long, she thought maybe the call had dropped.

"Jordan?" she asked.

# THE FALL OF BLACKSTONE MANSION

"Now."

## 22

Katherine slowed to a near stop when she saw Jordan's nauseating neon-blue Ferrari and the white van parked right in front of the mansion's gate. It surprised her, though, that she didn't see him or anyone else anywhere along the road leading up to it. *Where the hell are you?*

She parked, got out, and made her way toward the gate. She looked around, but didn't see anyone. "Guess he's in the house." She pushed the doors open and winced at their creak, a sound that she would have been delighted never to hear again.

"Kat," Jordan said.

She swung around to find him slipping out of the woods beyond his car. Despite what he'd done, he didn't carry an air of malice. His was one of anxiety and fear. *What is going on here?* She stomped toward him.

*Click click click!* The sounds occurred nearly simultaneously.

# THE FALL OF BLACKSTONE MANSION

She spotted the ten men in black emerging from both sides of the road. They surrounded her with aimed handguns.

"Please, Kat," Jordan said. "It'd be best if you kept your distance."

She held up her hands. Before saying anything else, she got a good look at the men. At this distance, she could finally clearly see their faces. Unlike what she'd suspected when she first saw one of them, they weren't wearing makeup. Their entire heads, except for their ears and the immediate area around their eyes, had been burned—she suspected ritually—and had scarred over. *This some kind of cult?* "It's you. All of you."

"You know them?" Jordan sounded like they'd left him out of a really fun game.

"Only from a distance."

The nearest one, to her left, whom she recognized as the tallest one she'd first seen in downtown Blackstone, at the Halloween party, and outside the Le Soleil club, spoke in a low, comforting, yet hissing voice. "Greetings, Ms. Norrington."

Katherine stepped back toward the gate.

"It's good to finally meet you," Mr. Low said.

"It was you, wasn't it?" Katherine asked. "Who sent those awful black roses to my hospital room? The note with that sick poem about Dean's death?"

Mr. Low nodded.

"How did you know all that about me?" Katherine asked.

One to her right, whom she recognized as the short one who'd searched for her in the streets around the Vista, spoke up with a higher, nasal voice. "We know a great many things, Ms. Norrington."

"What've you done with Kirk?"

"He's safe. Inside," Jordan said.

"We should join him, Ms. Norrington," said Mr. Nasal. "Time is of the essence."

"Did you bring the Key?" Mr. Low asked.

*The pendant.* She nodded and patted her purse.

"Mr. Blackstone?" Mr. Low asked.

Jordan walked up to Katherine and held out his hand.

*No! You can't have it! I won't let you!*

"Kat?" Jordan beckoned.

*No! It's mine! Mine!* She eyed Mr. Low.

He took a few steps toward her, aiming his gun directly at her head. "Ms. Norrington?"

She slid her purse off her shoulder. Her fingers grasped its strap with white knuckles.

"That's it," Jordan said.

*No! I won't let you!* Despite her intense internal objections, she placed the purse in his palm. "Flashlight's in there too."

"You won't need to worry about light, Ms. Norrington," Mr. Low said. "Shall we, Mr. Blackstone?"

# THE FALL OF BLACKSTONE MANSION

Jordan nodded at him, then pointed to the house and instructed Katherine, "Better go."

She turned around and headed up to the hill. Ever aware of the men in black's guns trained on her back, she kept her pace slow. "Who are they?" she asked Jordan.

"Some kinda secret society." Jordan sounded like he was thrilled to have held such knowledge. "Been around forever. For, like, thousands of years. Devoted to this place called the Realm. They say they're its guardians."

"I know what the Key is. Less sure about the Formula."

He shrugged. "Means by which they intend to use the Key to open the Realm."

"How long have you been working with them?"

"Not long. They found me shortly before Halloween."

*Sounds like about the time Miles's stupid friend Nigel blasted my pic of the pendant all over the goddamn internet.*

"Promised to unlock all the secrets of my great-grandfather's work. The Realm. Eternal life."

"And how's that going?"

"Seems the old man was eccentric, but not crazy. Extremely wealthy. Life was a party. Didn't want it to end. Got obsessed with prolonging it. Explored fringe medicine, spiritualism, all things esoteric. Finally, was able to track these guys down." He pointed his thumb back at the men in black. "They promised to share their secrets. He promised to fund it."

"So he built the mansion."

Jordan nodded. "It's some kinda gateway to this Realm thing. Not sure how the Formula works, but they're gonna show me."

"How do you know they're not gonna just kill us and take off with whatever?"

"We're not murderers, Ms. Norrington," Mr. Low said. "Not by choice."

Katherine paused and turned around. "You've got the pendant—Key. Lemme grab Kirk. We'll be outta your hair."

"You'll go straight to the authorities!" Mr. Nasal accused.

"They'd never believe me."

"Please, Ms. Norrington," Mr. Low said. "To the mansion."

Katherine continued on her way. She asked Jordan, "So why'd Marcus kill the family? Abandon the place?"

"I guess he needed them for the Formula."

*So, is it just the alignment of the family in their tombs to keep Silas alive? But he died long before they were even born.*

"I dunno why he abandoned the house. Maybe something went wrong."

# THE FALL OF BLACKSTONE MANSION

"You mean they haven't told you?" She threw a glance back at the men in black.

Jordan didn't answer her.

"Why did you hire me as your director?" she asked.

"They suggested it would distract you from learning too much about the mansion."

"That kinda backfired."

"Yeah, no kidding."

They reached the front doors. She was so used to entering on her own that she reached for the right doorknob.

"Please, allow me, Ms. Norrington." Mr. Low stepped past her and Jordan and opened the door for them.

Inside, Stacey was pacing back and forth. She stopped when she saw Katherine. "Kat!" She started to run for her when Mr. Low raised his hand to her.

"Patience, Ms. Webber," he said. "This will all be over soon."

Stacey eyed him. Her expression was one of revulsion rather than surprise.

*C's already met them? Probably all came out together.*

"Kat, I'm so sorry," Stacey pleaded. "I should've listened. It's just... Jordan's been so nice."

*Probably called him the second after Kirk and I left.* "It's okay, C. Let's just get through this."

"If you could please enter, Ms. Norrington, then we can do exactly that," Mr. Low said.

Passing Stacey, Katherine walked inside all the way to the sculptures of Artemis and Apollo. She turned around and waited as the rest joined her.

The men in black all turned on flashlights.

"Where's Kirk?" Katherine asked.

"Please. To Ms. Byrne's former resting place." Mr. Low pointed toward the west tower.

Katherine led the group to the tower's doors. Opening them, she saw no sign of Kirk. She glared at Mr. Low. "Where is he?"

Mr. Low nodded at the floor.

"Oh my God! Kirk!" Katherine shouted at the floor as if he could hear her through the feet of stone and concrete. She ran over to the tower's symbol, pressed it with both hands, and moved it to the left to unlock the tomb's door. As the rectangular section of stone receded from the rest of the wall, she barked at Jordan. "Make yourself useful." She lifted one hand from the symbol long enough to point to the other.

With an obsequious nod, Jordan took her place.

"Kat?" Kirk's voice echoed from out of the tomb's opening.

"Hold on, baby! I'm coming!" Katherine declared as she disappeared into the corridor. She raced down the steps in near complete darkness. She paused when she heard another set of footsteps scrambling up to meet her. She opened her arms wide and caught Kirk's lean torso. She squeezed him hard.

He kissed her several times. "Let's get outta here."

A light shone down on them as Mr. Low entered, the rest of the group directly behind him. "I'm afraid that's not possible."

"Why not?" Katherine demanded. "You've got the pendant! Hell, keep the whole purse! I don't care! What else could you need us for?"

"If you could please proceed, Ms. Norrington." Mr. Low pointed down the rest of the way.

Katherine took Kirk's arm and walked them down the steps.

"What's happening?" he asked her.

"Nothing good."

They reached the tomb's floor and walked around the coffin to the other side to stay as far away from the men in black as they could.

Mr. Low and the rest soon reached them. "Now then, Ms. Webber, if you could stand perfectly still, that will make this much easier."

Stacey asked, "What are you—?"

The other men in black surrounded her and bound her hands and feet.

"Stop!" Stacey screamed. "What are you doing? Jordan!"

"Let her go! She didn't do anything!" Katherine demanded.

Ignoring her, Mr. Nasal sealed Stacey's mouth with duct tape, then all of them hoisted her up and set her inside the coffin.

"Oh, my God. Are they really gonna...?" Kirk asked Katherine.

She nodded.

Stacey peered over at Kirk and resumed screaming into her gag.

"Please, Ms. Webber, remain calm," Mr. Low said.

"If she doesn't survive, people will come looking for her," Mr. Nasal warned.

Stacey screamed even louder.

"There's nothing to worry about. She'll most likely survive," Mr. Low assured. "And if she doesn't, she has no family. No friends. At least none who would miss her."

Stacey stopped screaming, glared at him, and swore. "Uh-ooh!"

A deep, wailing *groan* rose from the floor. A bitter chill swept over them. The stench of death embraced them. The telltale white spots appeared in the wall behind the men in black.

Mr. Nasal was the first to notice. "What's that?"

Mr. Low faced the wall. "Pay him no mind. He's powerless."

# THE FALL OF BLACKSTONE MANSION

With great exertion, Vernon's corpse-ghost dug out of the wall and bellowed at the men in black. Kirk shouted. Stacey screamed some more.

Ignoring the specter, Mr. Nasal approached Mr. Low. "I'm telling you, she's too distant a relation. The Formula won't work."

"It will." Mr. Low addressed Katherine. "Ms. Norrington, if you and Mr. Whitehead could please join us at the elder Mr. Blackstone's bust?"

Vernon's spirit descended on Stacey. On her binds. She screamed and screamed. As much as it tried, though, its ghostly, bony fingers merely passed through her.

Then, with a start, the apparition dissipated in a cloud of black smoke.

Mr. Low gestured for everyone to head back upstairs.

As Katherine passed Stacey, she assured her, "Hold on, C. I'll get you outta this!"

Reaching the ground floor, Katherine waited as the rest arrived.

Mr. Nasal relieved Jordan from his symbol-tending duties.

"Wait, you can't just leave C down there!" Jordan exclaimed.

The men in black ignored him.

Mr. Low pointed down the west-east hallway. "If you please, Ms. Norrington."

Not wanting to abandon Stacey, Katherine hesitated. "We can't just..."

"I assure you, Ms. Webber will be quite all right," Mr. Low reiterated.

"Not if you frickin' electrocute her, she won't!" Katherine shouted.

"Please, Ms. Norrington." Mr. Low again pointed down the hallway.

Katherine took Kirk's hand and led them out. Reaching Silas's bust, they waited for the rest to arrive.

"Gentlemen," Mr. Low said to the other men in black.

Including Mr. Nasal, four dispersed in separate directions, toward the other towers, Katherine assumed.

"Now, Ms. Norrington, if you could please?" Mr. Low pointed to the bust.

Katherine exhaled in frustration, not wanting to go through with this, but seeing no other option. She stood before the sculpture and went through the process of opening the corkscrew staircase hidden within.

They heard Vernon's distant wail, but Katherine detected a note of sad weakness. She suspected that as much as he might try, there really was nothing he could do.

# THE FALL OF BLACKSTONE MANSION

The moment the wall began to revolve, Mr. Low spoke with his creepy version of glee. "Excellent, Ms. Norrington. Now, if you please." He pointed down the steps.

As Katherine and Kirk descended, he asked her, "We're just gonna let them do this?"

"I'm open to suggestions."

"I might be able to overpower one."

"You'd only end up getting shot."

He grunted, conceding the point.

They soon arrived at the open space surrounding the wishing-well tower.

Mr. Low took a walkie-talkie out of his coat. "Are we in position, gentlemen?"

Four voices reported their confirmation.

"Then let us begin." Mr. Low approached the tower, his eyes fixed on its symbol.

They heard the same *grinding* sounds as they had when Katherine and Kirk's crew had activated the tower. In moments, the remaining circular staircase surrounding it began to lower.

"We're in, gentlemen," Mr. Low reported over his walkie-talkie. He then waited in silence at the top of the steps as all but Mr. Nasal arrived. "If you would do us the honor, Mr. Blackstone?"

Jordan stared at him, seeming not to understand what was being asked of him. He turned his gaze to Katherine.

"What are you looking at me for?" she asked.

"The Key, Mr. Blackstone," Mr. Low specified.

Jordan removed it from Katherine's purse and held it far in front of him as if it might bite. He lowered his foot onto the first step. He stopped and looked up at Katherine. "It's my birthright." He continued down.

Mr. Low nodded to Katherine. "If you please."

She and Kirk followed Jordan. The men in black were right behind them. They all met Jordan at the bottom.

He faced Mr. Low. "So I just…?"

Mr. Low nodded patiently. "As we instructed you, Mr. Blackstone."

"Okay." Jordan started the long walk around the central tower toward the lens apparatus.

Reaching the other side, they saw that a pale sliver of moonlight already stabbed out of the metal door's porthole, through the dusty shadows, through the lens, and splashed onto the singed south wall.

Jordan stopped with only a few feet to go. He faced the group. "So I…?"

"You're doing very well, Mr. Blackstone. Not long now," Mr. Low reassured him.

*For a guy so set on his birthright, he's not exactly exuding confidence. Probably knows what kind of hell we're about to unleash.*

# THE FALL OF BLACKSTONE MANSION

Jordan reached the apparatus and held up the Key. The ray of moonlight pierced it right below its top point. He set the Key in place. It fit perfectly with a *click*. "It's done," he called back to the group.

"Not quite, Mr. Blackstone, but soon." Mr. Low and his comrades sauntered over to Jordan, leaving Katherine and Kirk.

Katherine followed, with Kirk right behind. She was both curious about what was soon to happen and feeling the instinct to be ready for anything.

The ray of moonlight shining through both the Key and the lens swelled against the south wall until it formed a roughly oval, glowing shape of a pupil-free eye. The full moon was only seconds away.

"So soon." Mr. Low's gaze glued to the eye.

It had grown to a near-complete circle of moonlight.

Mr. Low took out his walkie-talkie. "On my mark."

A full, bright pale circle shone on the south wall. The moon's projection was so clear that Katherine was sure she could see a few craters.

"Now!" Mr. Low ordered.

They heard nothing nor saw anything change. No scraping stone. No clicking switches. No obvious changes in the projection.

*Did anything happen?*

A low *hum* and a distant *crackle*.

Katherine turned around. Her eyes snapped to the tower, first to the porthole, then to the silver band that ran the length of the ceiling to the apparatus.

Streaks of electricity shot along the band. Sparks showered from the regular junctions at which it had been attached to the ceiling. Odors of hot rust and burnt dust permeated the air.

"C!" Katherine shouted. While she couldn't stomach picturing Stacey, she was sure the charge they were witnessing was electrocuting her in the coffin of Eileen's former tomb.

"Quiet, Ms. Norrington!" Mr. Low declared. "It's almost done!"

Katherine returned her attention to the Key in its apparatus. Sparks exploded from it and rained down all around. The platinum vein glowed a soft yellow. "Oh, no."

A drop formed at the dead center of the circle of moonlight. It had the same color and consistency as mercury, except gravity had no effect on it. Dozens of sibling drops appeared all around the first one. They swelled like gorging silver maggots. Their number grew until they covered the entire surface within the circle with a rippling sheet of reflective liquid.

"What is *that*?" Kirk asked, in complete awe.

The ground shuddered.

"What's going on?" he asked.

## THE FALL OF BLACKSTONE MANSION

"Wish I knew!" Katherine said.

The most intense light exploded out of the circle's reflective sheet, enveloping it, and overwhelming the entire room in a solid beam of white.

Katherine, Kirk, and Jordan all twisted away to shield their eyes.

None of the men in black budged.

Katherine and Kirk dove behind the pillar to the right of the apparatus. Jordan dove behind the left one.

Pressing her fingers over her eyes, Katherine took a quick look at the men in black, at Mr. Low. She now saw the purpose of their sunglasses. They protected their eyes perfectly. *They knew this was gonna happen!*

"Such beauty!" Mr. Low declared. "After countless ages, the Realm is finally ours!"

He and his cohorts stared into the light for a few seconds.

Mr. Low jumped back on his walkie-talkie. "Success! Shut it down and join us."

The next second, the streaks of electricity vanished from the silver band in the ceiling. The showers of sparks ceased. The electrical current had cut off.

"Uh, hey, man, very pretty, but, uh, how does this all work for, ya know, me?" Jordan hobbled to Mr. Low while struggling to cover his eyes sufficiently.

Mr. Low kept his gaze on the light. "Patience, Mr. Blackstone!"

Jordan continued, "Yeah, it's just that, uh, you said—"

*Creak!* The sound came from behind them. Far behind.

*Is that the tower?* Katherine opened a tiny crack between her fingers. She was looking straight at the metal door to Silas's tomb.

*Creak!* The door's wheel turned one full revolution.

*Oh God, no!* "Kirk! We gotta move!" She snatched his hand and dragged him several yards away to squat against another pillar.

"What happened?" he asked.

"All hell's about to break loose!"

Mr. Nasal rounded the tower, standing only a few feet in front of its door. He pointed at the light. "Gentlemen! It's glorious!"

*Creak!* The door's wheel completed its final rotation.

Mr. Nasal turned around. "What's—?"

The door flew open.

## 23

A boot cobbled from the finest black leather stepped over the metal threshold that separated the mansion's crypt from Silas Blackstone's tomb. The charcoal cloth of the hand-tailored clothes rippled in the soft breeze. Silas's corpse swayed as it departed from his tomb. Except he didn't look dead at all. His skin shone with the vibrancy of a man who had just emerged from a cool mineral spring. The centers of his pupils glowed with the same ember red that Katherine had seen in the eye sockets of Eileen's and Vernon's ghosts. Tiny wisps of black smoke drifted out of Silas's ears, eyes, nostrils, and mouth, the corners of which turned up in a broad smile. His voice was deep, with a touch of raspy gravel. "At last!"

"Holy shit!" Jordan exclaimed.

Silas stepped forward three more feet when he noticed Mr. Nasal frozen before him. Silas smacked him aside. Mr. Nasal flew a dozen feet and crashed into a pillar with a nauseating *crack*.

He did not get up.

Silas shuffled forward like a toddler getting used to his first steps. He paused and *cracked* his neck. He let out a satisfied gasp and continued.

"What're you gonna do?" Jordan demanded of Mr. Low.

"What are *we* going to do?" Mr. Low asked. "We have the Realm. He's *your* ancestor." He then called to the others. "Gentlemen!"

He and the remaining men in black marched straight into the circle of light pulsating from the south wall.

"Well, somebody's gotta...!" Jordan ran up to Silas.

"Jordan, no!" Katherine called after him.

"Hey, jerkoff!" Jordan shouted at the old man.

Silas sniffed. "Such familiarity. The spawn of that vermin, Marcus?" He seized Jordan by the neck and snapped his head back like he was cracking open an oyster.

Jordan fell limp.

Silas sank his jaws into Jordan's throat and drank heartily. His Adam's apple bobbed up and down.

Jordan's flesh shriveled down to skin-wrapped bones.

Silas's head shot up. Another gasp. He wiped his mouth and dropped the husk of Jordan's body. "More!" The black wisps dissipated from his orifices. The heat faded from his pupils. His muscles toned.

# THE FALL OF BLACKSTONE MANSION

Color returned to his skin. He continued his forward march.

With her hands still covering her eyes, Katherine peered between her fingers and scanned the ground to see if there was something—anything—she could use as a weapon against this monstrosity. Across the room, she spotted her discarded purse. *Flashlight!* It wasn't much, but it was better than raw hand-to-hand.

She sprang to her feet and ran to her purse.

"Katherine, no!" Kirk shouted.

She sprinted past Silas's path and dove for her purse. Without the benefit of her hands covering her eyes, she fumbled with the cloth. Finally locating its opening, she tore out her flashlight and wrapped its strap around her wrist.

She jumped to her feet and swung around.

Silas was right there. "What is this? The curious little rodent sniffing around my beloved abode?"

"Go to hell!" Katherine struck him as hard as she could with the flashlight.

Silas's head snapped right back into place as if nothing had happened. "Now, that wasn't very kind." He seized her hand that gripped the flashlight and bent it backward.

*Craaack!* She could feel—and hear—the bones in her wrist shatter. She shrieked.

"No!" Kirk growled as he flew into them, knocking Katherine out of Silas's grip.

She hit the ground and slid an inch or two. Distracted by the terrible pain in her hand, she hollered and hollered.

"Well, what do we have here?" Silas asked Kirk, then lifted him several feet in the air and tossed him.

Katherine didn't see where Kirk landed. "Kirk! Kirk!"

Silas looked down at her and resumed his approach to finish her.

She scoured the ground again, but found nothing that could help her. Her eyes darted this way and that, desperate for anything.

The Key.

She felt the sudden, intense instinct to grasp it, wear it. She scrambled to her feet, leaving her flashlight behind, and booked for the apparatus. Reaching up, she plucked the Key and looked down at it. *I can't. I don't know what it'll do!*

She felt a stab of pain as a firm grip seized her shoulder. Silas spun her around. She struggled with the Key's chain.

He lifted her again. "Now, where had I left off?" He gripped her uninjured hand.

*Come on, Kat! Come on!* Her fingers wrestled with the chain, then finally managed a loose grip. She threw it over her head.

## THE FALL OF BLACKSTONE MANSION

Darkness cascaded all around her.

Freezing cold enveloped her whole body, just as it had in that strange place of the spirits' visions. She felt it everywhere, yet didn't shiver. As her eyes adjusted, she saw that, unlike in the ghostly realm, this reality wasn't one of shadows at all. It, in fact, looked the opposite of her own. The shining white circle was now a solid black disc. All highlights of gleaming metal and light gray stone had inverted into the darkest streaks and blots. All former shadows now shimmered silver, the same color as the moonlight that had reflected into the apparatus. Everything else, even her own appendages and Silas's whole body, had turned a misty gray.

*Silas! Why hasn't he done it?* She peered down at him, where his arm held her up.

He'd frozen.

No, not frozen, but moving very, very slowly.

She took a few breaths as she endeavored to understand her current circumstances. *Wait. Back at Sean's. I wonder...* She shoved Silas as hard as she could.

He didn't fly back as Ross had at the bar. He was moving too slowly for that. He did, though, start moving backwards and his grip on her was loosening.

She landed on her feet, watching him drift through the air. She knew she'd bought herself some time, but wasn't sure how much and also did not know the effect the Key would have on her.

She turned around and around, calling for Kirk, but heard no noise escape her lips. *Can he hear me?*

Out of the corner of her eye, she saw two bright shafts of light. As she watched them approach, she realized they were two humanoid figures. Closer still, she recognized them. They looked like the uncorrupted bodies of Vernon and Reginald at the point of their deaths. *It's their ghosts! How they look here!* She called to them, though she doubted they'd hear her with her soundless voice. *Vern! Reg!*

"Good evening, Katherine," Vernon said. "It's so good to finally meet you."

"We're so sorry it's been such a rough go," Reginald said.

"I've tried to reach out, tried to warn you..."

*Where's Gloria?*

"My dear wife passed on once Jordan had her remains buried in the family cemetery. Even returning them to the house didn't bring her spirit back."

"Would you like a hand with my dear great-grandfather?" Reginald asked.

*Yes! Thank you! Oh, no! Kirk!*

"He's over there, but you'd best hurry," Vernon warned.

She turned in the direction he was pointing.

# THE FALL OF BLACKSTONE MANSION

The black disc. She strode toward it and soon saw what Vernon was talking about. The disc was, in fact, an aperture to an infinite space, even the slightest glimpse into which froze her soul.

Silas had tossed Kirk directly into the aperture and, in Katherine's time frame, Kirk was slowly tumbling into the endless void beyond. She had a precious few seconds during which she could reach him and reel him back.

She peered into the aperture. It was an emptiness she couldn't fathom. Infinitely dark and expansive. Why the men in black so badly desired to escape into such a mind-shattering place, she had no idea.

But that wasn't the worst part. She caught out of her periphery that the aperture was closing. Slowly, but steadily. If she didn't hurry, it would trap Kirk inside forever.

She reached in. The chill was much like what she'd always felt around the spirits. She tried to grasp Kirk's hand, but it was several inches beyond her. She tried again and realized that if she stretched too far, she'd risk falling in herself.

*I have to wait.* The aperture would soon be small enough that she could brace against the surrounding wall, but in doing so, she risked missing her window to rescue Kirk.

She waited until the opening was small enough that she thought she could safely try another attempt.

"Katherine!" Vernon called from behind her.

She looked back to see Vernon and Reginald struggling with Silas. While he was strong, he wasn't so powerful that he could take them down without a fight. Foot by foot, the younger Blackstones were dragging Silas toward the Realm. *They're gonna toss him in!*

She reached in, snatched Kirk's hand, and yanked him out. They tumbled over each other until they landed flat on their backs. She sat up just in time to witness Vernon and Reginald stuff Silas into the abyss. The older man roared, but the aperture closed around him.

The Realm was gone.

Katherine jumped up. She eyed the two spirits, then Kirk. *Thank you! I—*

"Help him," Vernon said.

She tore off the Key. The world around her restored. She looked down. Kirk was still on his back, staring blankly at the ceiling. She turned around. Jordan's corpse lay several feet away. "How am I gonna...? Stacey!"

Shoving the Key in her pocket, she bent down to help Kirk to his feet. While his skin was cool, she felt

# THE FALL OF BLACKSTONE MANSION

a pulse. He was alive, just not responsive. "Come on, Kirk. We gotta go."

He said nothing.

She wrapped his arm around her and lifted him up with her legs. He was considerably heavier than her, so it was an actual struggle. She dug out her phone and tapped on its flashlight. She half walked, half dragged him toward the corkscrew staircase.

She felt a chill behind her. Kirk's weight eased. "Thanks, guys." Together, Katherine, Kirk, and the spirits of Vernon and Reginald made it to the staircase. She walked Kirk up to the surface. Turning toward the corridor to the rest of the house, she realized she'd forgotten the lever. She looked back. "Crap! I forgot the—"

The lever lowered by itself.

She smiled. "Thanks again." She walked Kirk all the way to the west-east hallway, then to the entryway hall. Reaching the staircase between the Artemis and Apollo statues, she eased Kirk down to the steps. She kissed his cheek. "I'll be right back. Gotta get C. Do *not* move."

He said nothing.

Katherine ran back through the house to the west tower. Arriving at the symbol, she suddenly realized, "I can't hold it down!"

The symbol pushed itself into the wall and slid to the left. The entrance to the tomb opened up. The scent of burnt flesh wafted out.

*Oh, God!* "Can you hold that?" she asked the Blackstone spirits.

They didn't answer.

Deciding that they could, she raced down the steps. Reaching the bottom, she called out, "Stacey? C? You still with me?"

A pained *groan* rose from the coffin.

Katherine ran to her. There Stacey lay, alive, but badly burned. "It's gonna be okay. Gonna get you the hell outta here." She located Stacey's feet and eased them out of their binds. She did the same for her hands, then warned her, "This part's gonna hurt. Ready?"

Stacey mumbled.

Katherine tore the duct tape off her mouth.

"Kat! Thank God! What...?" Stacey asked.

"Come on," Katherine said. "We gotta get you outta here." She helped Stacey out of the coffin and onto her feet. She walked her up the steps out of the tomb, being extra careful not to lead them off the edge of the staircase.

Exiting into the west tower, she heard the tomb's entrance close behind her. She walked Stacey all the way back to the entryway hall and sat her next to Kirk.

# THE FALL OF BLACKSTONE MANSION

"I can't get you both down at the same time, so, Kirk? I'm gonna walk Stacey down first since she's more injured," Katherine said.

"I'll be okay." But Stacey's voice sounded strained.

"No, we gotta get you down." Katherine helped her to her feet and walked her to the front doors.

A few feet before they reached them, the doors opened by themselves.

"Thanks, guys," Katherine said.

"Who are you thanking?" Stacey asked. "How'd the doors open?"

Katherine ignored her questions as they stepped into the moonlit night. They stumbled all the way down the hill. Katherine walked her out the gate to her car. She fished out her keys and opened the passenger's side door. On planting Stacey in the seat, Katherine finally got a good look at her skin.

Burns everywhere. At least first degree, probably some second, and who knew the extent of the internal damage? *I gotta get her to a damn hospital!*

But she couldn't right now, not with Kirk still back up at the mansion. "Hang on, C. Be right back." She ran up the hillside.

Reaching Kirk, she bent over to help him to his feet. "Baby, I'm here. Gonna get you out. Can you stand?"

He said nothing. He didn't move.

She reached out and lifted him up. She walked him toward the mansion's entrance. On crossing the threshold, she looked back into the house's darkness. "Vern? Reg? I'll get 'em to bury you so you can move on. Somehow." She walked Kirk out of the house.

A pair of sad, quiet creaks moaned behind her.

She paused and looked back. The front doors gently closed themselves. "Goodbye."

## 24

"Ms. Norrington?" the doctor asked.

"Yeah? How is she?" Katherine stroked the cast that now encased her injured wrist.

"Your friend's suffered quite a few burns, some second-degree. Also looks like she has some internal injuries, some hemorrhaging, but she'll pull through."

"Oh, thank God."

"We're prepping her for surgery now."

"Great. I mean, not great, but…"

"Your husband is a different matter."

"How so?" She didn't feel like correcting him as to her and Kirk's marital status.

"Well, there's absolutely nothing physically wrong with him."

"Okay?"

"But he's completely unresponsive. He won't answer any questions. Won't say anything at all."

"What's that mean?"

"Might be something psychological. Has he recently endured any severe trauma?"

*Yeah, but what do I call it? And why didn't I? The Key made me immune?* "Um, yeah."

"I'd like to keep him under observation for a few days."

"Of course. Can I see him?"

"Absolutely. Follow me."

He led her to Kirk's bed, where he lay still. Other than his blinking and breathing, she saw no movement. He didn't even look up at her as she entered.

"I'll leave you two alone," the doctor said.

"Thanks." She sat down next to Kirk. "Hey, baby? Can you hear me?"

He said nothing.

"Kirk, what happened in there?" she asked.

He said nothing.

"Please talk to me," she said. "I dunno how to help you if you don't talk to me."

He said nothing.

She took out her phone. "How about if I read to you? Something light. Wikipedia on the car-rental industry?" She didn't wait for him to respond as she started in on the article.

## THE FALL OF BLACKSTONE MANSION

"Miss?" a nurse asked.

Katherine sat up with a jolt. "Ah! Didn't realize I'd passed out." She found her phone in her lap and stuffed it into her pocket.

"Your friend's out of surgery if you'd like to visit."

Katherine stood. "Yeah, definitely. Can you...?" She pointed to Kirk.

"We'll monitor him."

Katherine followed the nurse to Stacey's room, where she found her almost completely bandaged from head to toe.

The nurse closed the curtain.

"How you doin'?" Katherine asked.

"Been better," Stacey muttered.

"Yeah."

"Kat? What *was* all that?"

"Best not to think about."

"I can't not think about it! My cousin stuck me in a weird-ass stone coffin and frickin' barbecued me!"

Katherine nodded. She had no idea what to say.

"Where is that prick, anyway? Gonna sue his ass so hard. Have him arrested for attempted murder."

"He didn't make it."

"What do you mean?"

"He was killed." *By his undead, billion-times-great grandfather!*

"How?"

"Doesn't matter."

"Oh. Well, so much for suing him."

"You know, C, you could maybe sue his estate."

"The one you're director of?"

"You're next of kin. You could probably..." Katherine shrugged.

"I'm listening."

---

"Ms. Norrington?" the doctor asked.

Katherine sat up in her chair next to Kirk's bed. She shuddered at the sight of the tubes crawling out of him. One for hydration, one for feeding, one for urination. She'd sat with him for the last two days and in that whole time, he hadn't said a word. "Yeah?"

"Let's step outside," the doctor said.

She followed him a few feet down the hall. "Any news?"

"This is an extremely strange case. Your husband hasn't slept."

"I know. I've been with him this whole time."

"I don't just mean this morning. I mean, since you arrived, he hasn't slept."

"At all?"

"We've kept very close observation. He hasn't even yawned."

"I don't understand. How's that possible?"

# THE FALL OF BLACKSTONE MANSION

"It's rare, but it is possible for humans under extreme traumatic stress to experience just as extreme insomnia. The thing is, if he doesn't start sleeping soon, he'll suffer very uncomfortable side effects."

"Like what?"

"Cognitive impairment. Hallucinations."

"Is there anything you can do?"

"We'll observe him for one more day, but if he doesn't sleep at all in the next twenty-four hours, I recommend medication."

"Okay. Thank you, doctor."

He nodded and went about his day.

She returned to Kirk's bedside and took his hand. "Kirk, baby? You gotta sleep. Please. Just close your eyes and relax."

His eyes remained open.

"Please," she said.

---

The following night, the doctor gave Kirk something he said would knock him out. Katherine wiped tears from her eyes as Kirk closed his.

"You should take a break," the nurse said.

"I don't wanna leave him," Katherine said.

"At least a walk."

Katherine eyed the direction of the front entrance. The chilly air did sound welcoming. With a nod, she headed out. She circled the parking lot once, then came back. Returning to Kirk's bed, it amazed her to see he wasn't there. His tubes hung loose.

She stepped into the hallway. "Kirk?" She didn't see him down the one end. Looking down the other, she found him trudging along toward the nurse's station. "Hey, Kirk? Can you hear me?"

He didn't respond.

She caught up to him just as he reached the nurse's station. "How you feeling?"

"Sir? Can I help you?" the nurse asked him.

He said nothing. His eyes were closed. His fingers reached down to the desk and crawled around like spider legs.

"Sir?" the nurse asked.

His left hand gripped a pen.

"Sir?" the nurse repeated.

"Baby, what are you doing?" Katherine asked. "What do you need? Talk to me."

Kirk said nothing. He didn't even look at her. He lifted his left hand and plunged the pen deep into his neck. Blood squirted everywhere.

The nurse smacked an alarm. "Got a code white!"

In two seconds, an army of other nurses surrounded Kirk and eased Katherine away.

"What did you give him? What's wrong with him?" Katherine demanded.

# THE FALL OF BLACKSTONE MANSION

Three nurses fought to hold Kirk while another removed the pen from his neck and hand. Another bandaged his wound as quickly as possible. The first three dragged him every inch back to his bed.

---

Katherine sat opposite the doctor in the reception area near Kirk's bed.

"We've had to restrain him and place him on suicide watch," the doctor said.

"I don't understand," Katherine said. "What's going on with him?"

"I've ordered a psych eval. We should know more in the next day. Until then, there's nothing else to do."

"Can I stay with him?"

"Kat, I'd suggest you go home. You've been here nearly a week. You need to get rest, do something other than hang out here."

"But I wanna—"

"I strongly urge you to take a break. I promise you we'll keep him safe."

She nodded, then collected her things, whispered goodbye to Kirk, and headed back to his apartment. Stepping inside, she realized the place felt foreign to her. She'd spent so much time at the hospital and before that, so much intense time at the mansion that a simple dwelling where she and Kirk had spent weeks together no longer felt like home. Especially without him.

She took out her phone and called her attorney.

"Hey, Kat. Been a minute. What's up?" Michael Roark answered.

"Hi, Mike. I'm in need of legal counsel."

She filled him in on Jordan's death, that of Mr. Nasal, and both Stacey's and Kirk's current conditions. She didn't give any details on the supernatural nature of the events, so he asked a lot of questions from what they were all doing in the mansion's crypt to how Jordan and Mr. Nasal had been killed, to how she, Stacey, and Kirk had escaped. To each she answered some version of "I don't know" or "It doesn't matter."

She made her request of Jordan's attorneys at Griffin+Miller. That they arrange to have the bodies of Jordan, Mr. Nasal, Reginald, and Vernon removed from the mansion. That Reginald and Vernon be buried in their designated graves in the family cemetery. That Jordan be buried next to them. That Mr. Nasal be left with the county. She didn't want to dump him in a ditch, but with no more information on his group, she had little choice.

That, as necessary, Griffin+Miller would coordinate with law enforcement to not hold any formal investigation into the deaths of Jordan or Mr. Nasal. That they'd simply be considered missing.

Stacey would then, as Jordan's next of kin, become the new sole beneficiary of his estate.

In exchange for Griffin+Miller's cooperation, Katherine and Stacey would agree never to mention any of this to anyone for the remainder of their lives. The firm and the estate would save face.

"I'll see what I can do," Michael said.

"Thanks, Mike." She hung up.

She then went to the bedroom and retrieved her laptop. Sitting on the couch, she started the first of many, many documentaries.

---

"The usual, hon?" Wendy asked Katherine.

Katherine's exhausted eyes lingered on the countertop. "No omelet. Just the uh..." She couldn't for the life of her remember what else the usual comprised. "The uh..."

"Hot cocoa?"

*Right! The sub-Swiss Miss sludge this place calls cocoa!*

"Mug'd be great."

"You doin' all right?"

Katherine wanted to be polite, but couldn't muster it. She shook her head. "Not really. Boyfriend's in the hospital."

Wendy leaned on the counter. "I'm so sorry to hear that. He gonna be okay?"

"I..." Katherine looked up at her. "I dunno. I hope."

"I'll put this in. On the house."

"No, Wendy. That's not necessary."

"It's a buck fifty, hon. We can cover it."

"Thanks."

Wendy smiled, nodded, and turned away to put in the order.

"Wendy?"

The older woman faced her.

"Thank you." Katherine could feel a tear roll down her cheek, so she dabbed it with a napkin. "For everything."

Wendy leaned on the countertop again. "You're outta here, ain't ya? Even if the beau gets better."

"How'd you know?"

"It's like I told you. Nobody moves to Blackstone. Either born here or married in. You were never meant to make it your home." She stood up straight. "I'll get you that cocoa."

---

"Kat?" the doctor asked over the phone.

"Hey, Dr. Eberwein," Katherine replied.

"Some good news."

"Kirk woke up?"

"Not yet, I'm afraid. Your friend Stacey is ready to be released."

It had been six weeks.

"Wonderful. Can I see her?" Katherine asked.

"Absolutely."

Katherine drove out to the hospital, arriving just in time to witness nurses discharging Stacey. She was looking much better, though Katherine imagined the psychological scars would take years to heal, assuming they ever would.

She accompanied Stacey as a nurse wheeled her out.

"It's so weird to be a friggin' multi millionaire!" Stacey practically shouted.

"I bet." Katherine smiled.

"Piles of cash! Pearl condo! Even a creaky Victorian! Know what I bought first?"

"Your own flower shop?"

"Ha! I ever have to see another flower, it'll be too frickin' soon. Nope. I ordered a ride back to my crappy studio."

As they exited the hospital, a black super stretch limo pulled up.

The chauffeur got out and greeted Stacey with a tip of his hat. "Ms. Webber?"

"That's me!" Stacey declared, pointing to herself.

"Whenever you're ready, ma'am," the chauffeur said.

Stacey looked up at Katherine. "I took care of your request."

"Thanks," Katherine said. "I think it's for the best."

Stacey stood up from her wheelchair. The chauffeur escorted her to the limo. She looked back at Katherine. "Don't be a stranger, Kat."

Katherine smiled, but had absolutely no intention of staying in touch with Stacey. While they'd endured an intense experience together, they barely knew each other, and Stacey only truly served as a reminder of whatever had happened to Kirk.

Katherine's phone vibrated in her pocket. She took it out and checked the ID. It was Joel Griffin.

"Hello, Mr. Griffin," she answered.

"Greetings, Ms. Norrington," he said with a tinge of annoyance in his voice.

"What can I do for you?"

"We've made all arrangements."

"Good to hear."

"There is the outstanding issue of the Key."

"What about it?"

"It seems to be missing. Do you have it?"

"What if I do?"

"I see. Some kind of insurance policy?"

"Call it that if you like."

"How do we know you won't take it to an appraiser, show it to the press?"

# THE FALL OF BLACKSTONE MANSION

*You're a little late for that first one.* "Guess you'll just have to trust me."

"Well, then, it looks like our business is concluded."

"Does look that way."

"Our best wishes to you and Ms. Webber."

"Thanks, Joel." She hung up, dropped her phone in her pocket, and entered the hospital. *Dean...* She marched straight to Kirk's nurse's station. "Any updates?"

The nurse shook her head. "Sorry, Kat."

Katherine nodded and left. *Could I contact Dean?*

---

"Hey, Dr. Eberwein, what's up?" Katherine asked him over the phone.

"Great news, Kat! Kirk's awake!" Dr. Eberwein announced.

Katherine drove over to the hospital as quickly as she could. She nearly parked outside of the lines, she was so eager to see him. She raced down the hall to his bed.

He was indeed awake, sitting up in bed, picking at a snack size fruit salad.

"Kirk!" she exploded and ran over to him, hugging and kissing him.

He didn't move a muscle.

"Oh, my God! I thought I'd lost you! I thought..." She noticed he wasn't reacting. "Hey, talk to me."

He set down his fruit salad and stared at her. His face was blank, as if he didn't recognize her at all.

"Kirk?" she asked.

Tears dripped out of the corners of his eyes.

"Hey. Talk to me," she pleaded.

"Kat... It... It was..." he collapsed into an ocean of sobs.

She held and rocked him. "It's okay, baby. We'll get you through this. We'll have our little adventure. No matter what it takes. No matter what it takes."

She touched her pocket, stroking the Key's edges protruding from within.

---

Coroners wheeled out four bodies from the entrance of Blackstone mansion. The instant the last gurney rolled onto the front steps, the everlasting twilight melted away to patchy morning sunlight streaming past the forest's branches and few remaining leaves.

Hours later, a demolition crew moved in. They left no wall, no tower, no door or window. They razed the once gloriously ostentatious black behemoth to a grand pile of broken stone, splintered wood, and shattered glass.

## THE FALL OF BLACKSTONE MANSION

Her rooms never to be inhabited again, her floors never to be trodden upon, Blackstone mansion was no more.

---

### THE END
### of
### *THE FALL OF BLACKSTONE MANSION*

Get your free book, *Zoe's Haunt*, by joining Augustine Pierce's newsletter. You can unsubscribe at any time.

# Acknowledgements

Thanks to my cover designers at MiblArt, who created a fantastic cover.

# DARK REALM

The Blackstone Trilogy

*The Haunting of Blackstone Mansion*
*The Possession of Blackstone Mansion*
*The Fall of Blackstone Mansion*

## Also by Augustine Pierce

*The Curse of Braddock Mansion*

Horror in Paradise

*Cenote*

*Arena*

*Down*

# About the Author

Augustine Pierce is the author of *The Curse of Braddock Mansion, Cenote, Zoe's Haunt, Arena, Down, The Haunting of Blackstone Mansion, The Possession of Blackstone Mansion*, and *The Fall of Blackstone Mansion*. He lives in Paris with his wife and collection of horror board games. He enjoys travel, snorkeling, and all things macabre.

Stay in touch! Subscribe to Augustine Pierce's newsletter and follow his Facebook page!

authoraugustinepierce@gmail.com

Printed in Great Britain
by Amazon

48581408R10162